ᴅescιɴy's

Tαroτ

Devil's Gate
Hunter's Season

Thea Harrison

Destiny's Tarot
Copyright © 2013 by Teddy Harrison LLC
ISBN 10: 0989972836
ISBN 13: 978-0-9899728-3-3

Cover Design © Angela Waters

Print Edition 1.0

Original publication in ebook format by Samhain Publishing:
Devil's Gate, 2012
Hunter's Season, 2012

devil's Gate

Chapter One

Sacrifice

Seremela Telemar leaned against the frame of the open balcony doors in her high-rise apartment and looked out at the ocean view. Tropical humidity licked her skin. As soon as she had gotten home, she had opened up the balcony doors, stripped off her work clothes and put on denim shorts and a tank top.

The weather in Miami was playing the blues. Like the singer Nina Simone's voice, it had a dark, sultry vibe with a bitter edge and an unexpected snap. Massive knots of moody clouds obscured the sun as they roiled over turbulent water, and heavy rain lashed down in vertical sheets. All that was needed was a world-weary man in a Bogart suit, fingering ivory piano keys in an abandoned hotel as he waited for a hurricane.

One of her head snakes slipped over her shoulder and rose to look at her, its jeweled gaze curious. It tasted the storm-laden air with a slender tongue. She put a forefinger underneath its jaw and nudged it gently. It slid closer and rested its tiny cheek against hers. In another mood, she might have smiled, but not this morning.

Was she really going to do this again?

Yes. Yes, she was.

She sighed, turned on her cell phone and hit speed dial. She held it up to her ear. A strained feminine voice on the other end said, "Serrie?"

"Yes," she said to her sister, Camilla. "I'll go get her."

"Oh, thank the gods," Camilla said fervently.

"I do not believe the gods are whom you should be thanking," said Seremela.

"Of course not!" Camilla said. "Thank you, Serrie! You know how much this means to me. Vetta won't mind me at all anymore—she never listens to anything I say, and I know what would happen if I tried to fetch her home myself. It would blow up into everything being my fault again, and the fight would drag on for hours and hours—and Vetta would make it as public as she could just to humiliate me, she knows how much I hate public altercations—"

"Camilla," Seremela said. Her tone was sharp enough that it cut through Camilla's babble. The other woman fell silent. She said, "I need for you to listen to me right now."

"Of course, whatever you need," Camilla said quickly.

"This is the last time I'm going to be able to drop everything to help fix your problems and your mistakes."

Camilla's tone turned cautious. "What do you mean, the last time?"

"I can't keep putting my life on hold every time something goes wrong for you, or every time you and

Vetta have an argument that you can't resolve. I just started a new, very demanding job. My employers are wonderful people, and they're really good to me, but there's only so much I can ask from them. Unlimited time off at a moment's notice is not one of those things."

Camilla's voice turned cold. "She's your niece. I thought you cared about what happened to her."

Seremela bit back her anger. Now it was time for the guilt trip, but it was always time for the guilt trip whenever she didn't do what Camilla wanted her to do, or say what Camilla wanted to hear. Children were rare for all of the Elder Races, and ever since Camilla had managed to carry Vetta to term, she had a skewed perspective on what the world owed her for achieving such a precious miracle.

"Of course I love both of you," she said. "And I care about what happens to you. That's why I'm agreeing to make this trip. But she's your daughter, and I have to agree, Vetta's out of control. You have to figure out how to work things out with her yourself. You need to get counseling, Camilla, not only for yourself but for Vetta too."

"I have to go," Camilla said.

Seremela rolled her eyes. "Sure you do," she said. She spoke too late, and a dial tone sounded in her ear. Camilla had hung up on her.

She resisted the urge to throw her iPhone. Instead she checked her work email again. Still no response from either of her new employers, Carling or Rune.

To be fair, she had only emailed them a short while ago, when she had gone into the office to ready her desk for a leave of absence. Deep regrets, family emergency, need to take time off work, will be in touch soon, blah blah blah. She had written the same kind of letter so often through the years, she could compose one in her sleep.

How many times had she sacrificed herself on the altar of Camilla's neediness? She blew out a breath. Too many times to count.

If she expected Camilla to learn to take responsibility for her own life, Seremela had to do the same. She had chosen to enable Camilla's behavior over the years. Now it was time to focus her energy on building a new life for herself.

After all, that's what her move to Miami was all about: taking on a new job and doing medical research she really wanted to do, building a new life and exploring new opportunities and horizons. It was not too late for her to break out of her sheltered, academic shell.

The small, poisonous voice of her Adversary whispered, the only confidence you ever found was in the classroom or the laboratory. When you're not lecturing over an autopsied body, you turn into a klutzy fool. You haven't dated in years—actually decades now—and you rarely make new friends. You're never going to have children of your own, and you've grown set in your ways as well. You're starting a new life with the old you. All your old problems and old weaknesses have come with you, so how can you expect to truly change anything?

She rubbed her forehead tiredly. The medusae believed that each medusa was born with a drop of poison in their souls. The poison turned into the medusa's Adversary, the dark voice that whispered doubts and fears in one's own thoughts. The measure of one's strength was determined by how well one withstood one's internal Adversary. Seremela tried to overcome that negative voice, but her own Adversary had a lot of ammunition to use against her.

She forced herself to concentrate on the task at hand. There was no reason to procrastinate any longer by pretending that she was waiting to hear back from her bosses. Many employers were very understanding about family emergencies—at least the first time. And Carling and Rune were much better than many other employers. They had gone out of their way to show her how much they valued her.

She sighed, tossed her phone onto the coffee table and went to pack a carry-on. Seriously, when she found Vetta, she was going to wring that girl's neck. That'd solve any potential problems with further confrontation or conflict. It wouldn't cure Camilla of her neediness or get Seremela a life outside of work, but that was okay, it would make room for taking care of the rest. Lots and lots of lovely room.

A knock sounded on her apartment door. The nictating membrane on her eyes snapped shut in surprise, and she paused, bras clutched in one hand and undies in the other. Dropping the filmy, colorful handfuls of underwear into her open case, she hurried to the door and peered out the peephole.

A dark haired man stood on the other side of her door, looking like he had just stepped out of an issue of GQ magazine. He stood in a casual stance, hands in the pockets of a hand-stitched linen summer suit, the jacket unbuttoned. Every expensive line of the tailored clothes emphasized his lean, well shaped body. His sleek dark hair, layered in a razor cut, fell on his forehead as though he had just run his fingers through it. His eyes were just as dark as his hair and glittered with intelligence. In contrast his skin was the pale ivory of a man who never saw any sunlight.

Because if he did, he would vanish in a blaze of fire.

Duncan Turner, internationally famous lawyer and the youngest progeny of one of the most Powerful Vampyres in the world, stood on her doorstep? In midmorning?

Once her nictating membranes started they wouldn't stop. They snapped open. Shut again. Open again. Shut again. It was a medusa's version of nervous hiccups.

She jerked her head back and rubbed at her eyes quickly to make them stop.

When she opened her eyes again, she saw that several of her snakes were trying to look through the peephole, pushing each other out of the way.

She grabbed at her snakes, gathering them up frantically. They kept sliding out of her hands, trying to get back to the peephole.

Forget about dating. *This is why I don't play poker,* she thought. *Because I have so many tells, and they're all so opinionated.*

Duncan knocked on the door again, making her jump. "Seremela?" he called. "Are you home?"

Even through the door, his rich, baritone voice sent shivers down her skin. Her agitation sent all her snakes undulating.

For crying out loud, stop it! she told them telepathically. Out loud, she said, "Yes, I—I'm home! Hold on just a moment. I'll be right with you!"

Now all of her snakes were trying to look out the door. They knew Duncan was outside too. They liked Duncan. A lot.

"Calm down, damn it," she hissed out loud.

As usual, they ignored her. Some elderly medusae were famous for their control over their head snakes, and everything they did or said was a graceful symphony of coordinated movement.

Not Seremela. Oh no, hers never paid attention to a word she said to them, and she had long since given up hope of exerting any true control over them. They were like a pack of poorly trained poodles.

"Seremela?" Duncan said.

He sounded…complex, but then he always sounded complex, the flavors and notes in his voice as layered as a fine, aged wine. He was a master of nuance and one of the sharpest legal minds in the world, and—and she admired him so damn much, it tied her up in knots.

And it didn't help in the slightest that his voice, like actors Alan Rickman or Liam Neeson, was spellbindingly beautiful. According to Carling, Duncan rarely made court appearances any longer, but when he did, other lawyers, judges and legal professionals from different demesnes traveled from all over the world just to hear him speak.

Now he sounded divided between amusement and worry.

"Everything's all right," she called out as she patted the door. That was a stupid thing to say, especially in the face of her family emergency. If she could, she would climb in bed and pull the covers over her head. Over all their heads. "You just caught me by surprise. Hold on a moment."

"Take your time," he said.

His voice. Swear to gods, she was pretty sure he could bring her to orgasm just by talking.

That thought did nothing to help her present a cool, collected attitude of her own, nor did it help to calm down her excited little head freaks. She threw up her hands and dashed across the apartment, back to her bedroom where she grabbed a scarf and wound it around the snakes with quick expertise, starting at the back of her head.

The normal life span for medusae was around 450-500 years, and their snakes grew longer and more poisonous as they aged. Infants and small children had snakes as small as their fingers, the poison from their bites about as irritating as a mosquito bite, while elders had snakes that often trailed a foot or so along the ground. A single bite from the snake of an elder could make a grown human very sick, and multiple bites would cause almost certain death to several races.

Seremela was in late middle age, close to 380 years old, and her snakes reached past her hips. She had never felt threatened or afraid enough to cause her snakes to bite anyone. She pulled the mass over one shoulder and worked quickly down their length.

They did not want to be wrapped in the scarf—really, it was like putting children down for a nap—and their agitation increased until she had them all snugly under cover and eased them back over her shoulder again. Once they were tucked in a warm, dark place, they went quiet. Even as she stepped out of the bedroom, she could sense that they were asleep.

She took a deep breath and hurried back to open the door. Duncan, who stood looking down the hall as he waited, turned back quickly to face her. His dark, clever gaze regarded her for a moment. She felt her cheeks grow warm at the open concern in his expression.

She held the door open wider, more to give herself an excuse to back away from his penetrating, too observant attention than to be hospitable, although she did manage to say, "Please, do come in."

"Thank you." Hands still tucked in his pockets, Duncan strolled into her apartment.

Her mouth dried as she watched him. In some ways he looked so normal. At five foot ten or so, he stood just a few inches taller than she did. And he wasn't oversized.

He had a neat, compact build, and when he moved something unique and intangible became manifest, as his sharp, quiet intelligence flowed through his body.

All Vampyres had the same liquid, inhuman grace, but not all of them affected Seremela the same way that Duncan did. She ducked her head and shut the door. When she turned around to face him, she found him studying her again. She grew even more self-conscious, too aware of the amount of bare skin exposed by the skimpy, thin material of her red tank top and her shorts. Her toenails were painted a bright, saucy lime green. She glanced down at her bare legs then back up at him.

If only she had her work clothes on, and a dissected corpse on a table between them. Then she would know what to say and how to act.

Still, she had to start somewhere. She said, "I wasn't expecting company."

"I hope you don't mind that I stopped by unannounced," he said.

His voice moved over her in an invisible caress. She shivered as her mind supplied her with images garnered from her earlier storm-washed fancy:

Duncan, dressed in a Bogart suit, stroking long, clever fingers on piano keys, with his dark head bent and a melancholy gaze. Then she steps into the room and he turns to her with fierce joy—giving her a look that says they are the only two people in the world—

Heavy reality thudded into place around her. Gah. Where were they? Oh, he had said something. That meant it was her turn, right? Argh, where was a dead body when you needed one the most? She fumbled for an appropriate response. "No, of course not."

His gaze had lingered at her head. He gave her a small, grave smile. "I'm sorry to see the little rascals are tucked away today."

Warmed, she touched the back of her head with a self-conscious hand. Many people were afraid or repulsed by a medusa's snakes, and at various times throughout history, medusae had been persecuted and killed because of it. The most famous example of a medusa being murdered was in ancient Greece, when Perseus had beheaded a woman who was supposedly so ugly, the sight of her could turn people into stone.

But Duncan wasn't like most other people. He seemed to enjoy the snakes, and he had treated them with indulgent amusement when they had flirted with him at Carling and Rune's winter solstice Masque party.

Her snakes didn't have the slightest problem with social situations—not that they ever behaved appropriately.

Once at a work party, she grew lightheaded and extremely giddy while she talked with the woman who was her boss at that time. When she turned around, she caught several of her snakes lapping at leftover alcohol in the bottom of several glasses on a table behind her. Thankfully her boss had been amused and helped to call her a cab ride home.

"They needed a time out," she confessed. "What a surprise to see you, Duncan, especially in the middle of the day."

His smile widened briefly before it disappeared. He said, "I remembered the layout of your apartment building and the basement garage from when I dropped you off after the Masque party. It's a simple matter to park in the garage and come up the elevator, and the windows at the end of the hallway are quite easy to avoid. This building is very Vampyre friendly."

"I see," she said.

Duncan drove a silver Aston Martin V12 Zagato with windows that had been tinted with full spectrum UV protection. The price tag on the car had to be well in excess of half a million dollars, but when you were the founding partner of one of the premiere law firms in the United States that specialized in Elder Races inter demesne law, you could afford some unusually nice perks.

She glanced at the open balcony doors that led out to a wide patio. Not only did she and Duncan stand well away from them, but it was still dark outside and raining hard. Even though her apartment faced the east, there wasn't any danger of sunshine streaming in the windows until the storm blew away.

No doubt Duncan had already calculated all of that even as he stepped inside her apartment. For him, any contact with the sun would be excruciating and would turn lethal within a matter of seconds. He must be aware of the sun's position every moment of his life.

She turned back to him and met his gaze. "What can I do for you?"

"I'm butting in where I haven't been invited, Seremela," he said bluntly. "And I hope you forgive me for it. I happened to be in a meeting with Carling when she received your email. I know you have a family emergency, and I wanted to stop by to make sure you were okay."

Her lips parted and her eyes widened. She had left her medical examiner position in Illinois and moved to Miami to focus on private medical research for Carling and Rune. Ever since then she had enjoyed getting to know Duncan.

Duncan was Carling's youngest progeny, and as Carling and Rune's lawyer, he was working closely with them on setting up their new agency. Seremela was one of the agency's first employees.

Duncan wasn't Seremela's boss, by any means, but he would be aware of any administrative decisions Carling and Rune made, and they certainly wouldn't hesitate to mention confidential matters to him.

As their group was small and most were new to the area, they tended to socialize together as well as work together. Seremela and Duncan had shared good conversations at group events, and she had hoped they might have begun to develop a friendship, but coming in person to check on her wellbeing went beyond anything she could have expected.

He cocked his head. "Are you okay?" he asked gently. "You haven't had a death in the family, have you?"

"No!" she blurted out. "No, I haven't. Duncan, I— this was so thoughtful of you. Thank you."

"Oh, good," he said. The set of his shoulders eased, and he gave her that crooked smile of his that was so damn charming. "Nobody has died, and you aren't angry with me for intruding. I count both those things as wins. Do you mind me asking what has happened? We're all transplants to Miami, and it's all too possible to feel cut-off and alone. Carling and I were both concerned you might need help but not feel comfortable enough to ask for it."

She groaned and gestured. "I just found out my niece ran away from home a few months ago. My sister has kept it under wraps all this time. She hired a detective to find Vetta—that's my niece—and now that he has tracked her down, we need to bring her home."

Duncan's gaze had grown intent as she talked. "I take it your niece is all right?"

"Yes, as far as I understand, she is," Seremela said. "That girl's got a talent for finding trouble though, and if she can't find trouble, often she'll create it. I'm afraid I can't talk with you long. I'm on standby, and I'm getting ready to leave for the airport so I can take the first available flight out."

"Your sister must be grateful you're going with her to get Vetta."

Seremela shook her head. "Oh, my sister's not going to get Vetta."

Duncan's sleek dark brows lowered. "Excuse me?"

Seremela gave him a dry look. "Camilla can't face conflict," she explained. "I'm going to get Vetta by myself."

His frown deepened. "Forgive me again," he said. "I'm well aware of how intrusive this might seem, but I do not like the sound of that."

"Well, it is what it is." She twitched a shoulder. "Although I know how irritating that statement is to a lot of people too. Right now the most important thing is to get Vetta home safely, and that means moving as quickly as possible now that we know where she is. Everything else can be dealt with later."

As she talked, Duncan turned to look out the open balcony door. She didn't mind in the slightest. It gave her the opportunity to study his profile.

Slight lines carved the corners of his eyes and his expressive, well formed mouth. He must have been around thirty when Carling turned him at the height of the California Gold Rush in the mid nineteenth century.

While he would forever wear a young man's face, there were subtle telltale signs that spoke otherwise. He carried a certain gravitas in his presence that simply didn't exist in younger men. Somehow it held the weight of years and experience without seeming too heavy.

Oh, she did like him, so much. She twisted her fingers together and offered, "I also thought about asking the detective if he would go with me when I went to get her."

Duncan pursed his mouth. The small, thoughtful expression hollowed already lean cheeks and accentuated the strong line of his cheekbones. "Most detectives won't get physically involved, especially if it involves a family matter," he said. "The majority of detectives work on divorce documentation, do background checks and that sort of thing."

"I know," she said quietly. She had also thought about hiring someone who specialized in extracting people from cults, drugs and other subversive cultures. She just wasn't sure any professional interventionist would agree to handle something as trivial as Vetta's sheer bloody mindedness.

Vetta wasn't addicted or brain washed. She was just contrary to the bone. She was also twenty, which was especially unfortunate since that was well past the age of consent in most jurisdictions. Medusae aged so much more slowly than humans, and Vetta's emotional maturity was more like a young human teenager's than a grown adult.

"Where is your niece now?" he asked, glancing at her.

She closed her eyes and sighed. "She's at Devil's Gate."

"Devil's Gate?" He pivoted sharply to face her.

"I see you know of it," she said, her voice flat.

"Of course I know of it," he said. "Bloody hell."

Chapter Two

Law

D evil's Gate. Yes, Duncan knew of it.

That period of his life was etched indelibly in his mind. He had lived his last days as a human and his first nights as a Vampyre during the riotous Gold Rush in San Francisco. He would wake in the evenings, starving for fresh blood and newspapers. Gods, he had loved that time. It had been wild, greedy and anarchistic, and everyone had been a sculptor, carving out their futures and fortunes the best way they knew how.

He had followed the original news about Devil's Gate in the *Pacific Courier*. In June of 1850, a gold nugget had been discovered at Devil's Gate, which lay just north of Silver City in western Nevada. For ten years the entire area became the scene of frenetic mining. The gold rush in Nevada had been even wilder than the California Gold Rush, fueled by a thread of land magic that ran like liquid mercury throughout the desert mountains and rock.

Formed out of lava rock, Devil's Gate itself had been blasted wider to create a toll road on the route to Virginia City. The narrow opening soon became notorious as a popular hideout for highwayman, and anyone who wanted to pass along the route safely had to travel armed.

Even with the last hundred and sixty years of searching and with modern surveying techniques, it was still possible today to stumble upon a vein of magic-rich metal. In eastern Nevada, the Nirvana Silver Mining Company had done just that when they had accidentally blasted open a passageway to a small pocket of Other land that held a magic-rich silver node.

A few months ago, in March, the news of the discovery had slammed through the media. The law was very clear about mining rights and ownership in Other lands. Even though the passageway was on the Nirvana company grounds, and even though there were no indigenous people living in the Other land, the mining company had no legal right to harvest the newfound vein of silver.

Succumbing to greed, the company owner had imported undocumented workers and held them against their will, forcing them to work in such inhumane circumstances that several had died. An Elder tribunal Peacekeeper on a routine mission had uncovered the crimes.

The magic that ran through the rock in Devil's Gate had never led to a full crossover passageway—at least not one that had ever been discovered or documented. But after what happened in Nirvana, that slight spark of land magic had been enough to ignite the imaginations of a great many people.

After all, if a crossover passageway leading to a magic-rich silver node could be uncovered so recently in Nirvana, who knows what one could discover in the witchy land at Devil's Gate? Perhaps there were slivers of previously undiscovered magic-rich gold, or there might be more silver, or even more buried passageways that led to Other lands.

Thousands of people, both Elder Races and humankind, converged upon the place. They chased gold and silver, magic and fool's dreams of sudden wealth.

Almost overnight a sprawling city of tents and RVs sprang up in Gold Canyon. By mid-April, nearly sixty thousand people had struck camp. At the end of May, the tent city had grown to over twice that size. Desperate for opportunity and a fresh start, illegal immigrants poured north from Mexico, while charlatans and schemers, sightseers, prostitutes, drug dealers and thieves poured in from all over the globe, creating a brawling mess that grew messier and more violent as the summer solstice came closer and the desert temperatures escalated accordingly.

The State of Nevada was caught completely off guard. Lawmakers struggled to come up with an effective way to deal with the situation, their resources already severely overburdened from a long economic downturn. They didn't have the manpower to police an entirely new city that had sprung up overnight.

The last Duncan had heard, the state had filed several appeals for help, with the Nightkind demesne in

California, with the Demonkind demesne in Texas, and with the human Federal government.

The process had stalled under one essential question: under whose jurisdiction did the very expensive problem fall? If more than fifty percent of the population in the tent city were creatures of the Elder Races, then the jurisdiction—and responsibility for policing it—fell to the Elder Races demesnes. But nobody could answer the question, because nobody had conducted a Census. There hadn't been time.

And Seremela intended to walk all alone into that cesspool?

Duncan's jaw tightened as he looked down into her face. "This won't do, Seremela," he said, and this time he didn't even bother with an apology for intruding. Determination hardened his face and body. "It won't do at all."

A spark of amusement had entered her colorful, intelligent gaze. "If by 'it won't do,' you mean that Vetta can't be allowed to wreak havoc on the thousands of unsuspecting people at Devil's Gate, you would be right," she said. "That girl is like water running downhill. She can find the lowest common denominator in just about any situation."

"I think you know very well that's not what I meant," he said.

He had not met many medusae before her. They were rare, comprising only a small fraction of the Demonkind population, and they also tended to be rather clannish.

Seremela was strange to him, and lovely, with fine-boned, feminine features and blue-green eyes that had vertical slits for pupils. She seemed on the small side for a medusa, which was around average height for a human woman, with a trim waist and rounded breasts and hips. Her skin was a pale creamy green that had a faint iridescent pattern that resembled the pattern on snakeskin, but he had touched her hand before on other occasions, and her warm soft skin felt entirely human. He loved her exotic beauty. Her snakes were frankly mischievous, and he loved them as well.

Most of all what drew him to her was her intelligence and her gentle nature.

She was a medical doctor, a pathologist and an academician. Her snakes were poisonous, which did give her beauty a certain edge, but many creatures, like himself, were immune to their poison.

And in any case, she would have to be caught in a situation extreme enough that her snakes felt threatened to bite. Even the most quickly acting poisons took at least a few moments to act. In a physical struggle, those few moments could easily mean the difference between life or death.

She could be deadly, but she was also very vulnerable.

Unable to resist, he reached out to take her hand, and she let him. He relished the sense of her slender warm fingers resting in his grip. She kept her neat, oval fingernails trimmed close, a practical choice for a medical examiner turned researcher. "You can't go to Devil's Gate all by yourself. It's too dangerous."

She did not protest nor did she appear to be angry at his presumptuous language. Instead, she stared at their hands as she pointed out, "My niece is there all by herself."

"Which, we can both agree, is not acceptable," he said.

The smile in her eyes dimmed, her expression tightened and she looked at the floor. "Well, there isn't any other option," she told him. "I spent half the night and much of this morning trying to figure out the best thing to do."

"There has to be some other way," he said.

"There isn't," she said, her voice turning flat again. "There's no legal recourse. The state can't even keep the area adequately policed. They certainly don't have the resources to send anyone in to find one person who I can guarantee doesn't want to be found. And frankly, I don't want to bully my sister into going with me. She'd only wring her hands, fall apart and be useless. Trust me, that would be much more trouble than it's worth."

"I understand," he said. He raised her hand and pressed his lips against her fingers. She froze, her startled gaze flashing back up to his. "But nevertheless I still can't let you go to Devil's Gate by yourself."

This time she did pick up on his language. "You can't let me," she repeated with a careful lack of emphasis.

He knew exactly what it sounded like, and he was entirely unrepentant for it. He stressed, "Not by yourself, Seremela."

Her shoulders drooped and she tried to pull her hand out of his. "While I understand that you mean well, I don't have time to argue with you," she said. "My taxi's coming in less than a half an hour, and I'm not finished packing yet."

"Cancel it," he told her, his fingers tightening on hers.

"Duncan-"

He pulled her closer until they stood toe to toe, and he looked deeply into her strange, beautiful eyes. "Cancel it," he repeated. "And take your time as you finish packing. I will sort out the quickest flight to Reno then come back to pick you up."

He could see from her puzzled expression that she still didn't quite get it. "I'm not sure what to say."

In light of the number of clues he had dropped, her confusion seemed remarkably innocent and was entirely adorable. He raised an eyebrow. "You don't have to say anything," he said. "Or better yet, figure it out while you finish packing. You can tell me whatever it is on the flight, since I'm coming with you." A delicious warm rose color washed intoxicatingly underneath her creamy light green skin. "You are?"

"I am. Now, don't argue with me," he said as she took in a quick breath. He began to wonder just how far she would let him push her. In wondering where her boundaries might be, and what she might do should he cross them, he began to enjoy her even more than he had before. "Just do as I say."

She shut her mouth with an audible click. "Can't. Won't. Don't. You've used a lot of archaic-sounding prohibitives in the last fifteen minutes."

He could tell she wasn't really angry. She was, ever so gently, warning him not to go too far. It pleased him so much he ran the tip of a finger very lightly down her cheek. "You might have noticed, my dear," he murmured. "I happen to be a nineteenth century kind of a guy."

He left her sputtering and rosier than ever, and he spent a pleasant ride in the elevator to the basement garage wondering what she would say to him when he picked her up. A few minutes later, he called Carling and Rune's house. Rune picked up.

Carling was a Vampyre, but Rune wasn't. Rune was Wyr, and just under a year ago he had been First sentinel for Dragos Cuelebre, Lord of the Wyr in New York, until he had mated with Carling. Rune and Carling had relocated to Miami, and for several months they had been gathering underutilized talent from across several different demesnes.

Now Rune and Carling were setting up an international consulting agency so that they could put to use the talent they had gathered around them. Some parts of the agency, such as consultations with the Oracle, would be operated on a sliding scale fee, and other parts would be profit-based only. Carling must have told Rune about

Seremela's email, or perhaps Rune had read it for himself.

"Seremela and I need to fly to Reno," Duncan told Carling's mate.

"Yo-okay," said Rune. "Duncan, you dog."

"You had to go there," Duncan said. He smiled to himself as he negotiated the afternoon traffic. He liked Rune. They had learned to work well together when they had traveled to the Dark Fae Other land of Adriyel to see Niniane Lorelle safely to her coronation as the Dark Fae Queen.

"Seriously, is everything all right?"

"I hope so. Seremela has a runaway niece who has ended up at Devil's Gate, of all places." He paused briefly as he listened to Rune mutter a curse. "We're going to extract her from the situation and escort her home to her mother."

"Anything we can do?"

One of the first acquisitions their brand new consulting agency had purchased was a private jet that could seat up to twelve people and that had the capacity for international travel. They were serious about the agency and were allocating enough money to set it up with top notch resources.

Of course Duncan was well aware that the plane also had the capacity to travel quite comfortably across the continental U.S.

"It would be nice," Duncan said, "to get to Nevada as quickly as possible before her niece has a chance to get hurt."

"Is this urgent enough to bargain away a favor to a Djinn?"

Duncan gave the question serious consideration. Most people had never even met a Djinn. Still fewer were able to draw a Djinn's attention long enough to bargain with one. Duncan and Seremela were acquainted with Khalil and could talk with him, but Khalil's Djinn sensibilities were such that he would probably see nothing wrong with bargaining with them for a favor in return. While the situation at Devil's Gate was unsafe and volatile, owing a favor to a Djinn could be an expensive and even more dangerous business over the long haul.

He said, "I don't think so. Still, we should get there quickly."

"I'll have the plane fueled and on the tarmac inside an hour," Rune said.

"Thanks, I appreciate it."

"I wish Seremela had felt comfortable enough to ask us herself."

"Borrowing a plane is quite a big favor to ask, Rune," Duncan told him. "And she's new to Miami and still feeling her way. Hell, we all are. It's just that some of us have known each other longer than others. Give her time."

"Good point. Let us know if there's anything else we can do."

"Will do." Duncan ended the call.

He was frowning when he reached his fifteen thousand square foot house. He would pack two bags. One of them would be a backpack filled with weapons, cash, a few toiletries and ways to keep himself protected from the sun. That would be the essential bag.

The other would be filled with luxuries like extra clothing, along with a securely encrypted laptop in case he found some time to get some work done. While he would also definitely pack a satellite phone as well, the land magic around Devil's Gate interfered with phone reception so they would have to plan on being self-sufficient.

They would have to drive to Devil's Gate from Reno, which meant they needed to rent an SUV. He made more calls to arrange a rental, including camping supplies, food and water for Seremela, and several cases of bloodwine. He tried to rent an RV, but there weren't any available on short notice within five hundred miles of Devil's Gate.

If retrieving Seremela's niece took longer than a few days, and if anything happened to his food supply, he would have to hunt for sustenance. Hopefully he would be able to find and pay for willing donors. If not, he would do what he had to do. He thought of the delectable healthy blush that had risen in Seremela's cheeks, and rather to his shock, his cock hardened in response.

He was an intelligent, educated and mature man who believed in law, in self control, and in regulating his emotions. He did not mix his appetites or confuse hunger for sustenance with sexual desire. He would not be that inconsiderate, either to his donors or to his lovers. Not even when a chaotic, sexy harpy had offered him a chance to taste her rare blood in exchange for sex had he given in to temptation.

But he also knew there were places and times where the law did not reach, and Devil's Gate was one of those places and one of those times. Apparently there were also times when a man's appetites became mixed, no matter how much self control he might try to exert over himself.

It had been some time since Duncan had done so, but he knew how to navigate through lawlessness. In fact he was looking forward to it again, and while he would have helped Seremela for decency's sake, no matter what, it certainly did not hurt in the slightest that she was so very beautiful, and he was intensely attracted to her.

No doubt she would be very grateful for everything he did. She might even offer to feed him, herself.

If she did, despite all of his carefully thought out principles, he would take what she offered. Hell, he would jump at the chance. His cock grew even harder as he thought of her bare, slender neck arched in invitation. He thought of sinking his teeth into her soft skin while her breasts filled his hands, and his erection grew so tight it became painful.

Oh, Duncan, he thought. You had to go there too, didn't you? Rune had been teasing, but he'd also had the right of it. You are a lowdown dirty dog.

Chapter Three

The Dance

While Seremela waffled over what to pack, her iPhone pinged. She hurried into the living room to snatch it up from the coffee table.

She had received a text from Duncan. *Everything is set. We have transportation to Reno, also an SUV with supplies. I'll be there at noon to pick you up.*

An invisible weight lifted from her shoulders. She was intelligent and capable. She could have arranged transport. She could have retrieved Vetta on her own. But the fact that she didn't have to, that she had the kind of emotional support that Duncan had so generously offered her, was indescribably wonderful. It spoke of serious caring, and friendship.

The fact that she also found him heart-stoppingly sexy shouldn't factor into her thinking at all. She should be focused on the task itself, which was ensuring that her niece got home safely—whether Vetta wanted to or not.

And Seremela would be focused on the task, when it really mattered. For now, she felt young, and feeling that way at nearly four hundred years old was a kick. Her pulse raced like a giddy schoolgirl's.

She and Duncan would have hours of time alone. She could watch him in secret. Sometimes he would smile at her in that slightly crooked self-deprecating way that he had. He would talk with her, combining his intelligence with the sound of his gorgeous voice in a way that was so seductive to her. They might have as much as two or three days together. It seemed an extravagant fortune in stolen time.

Carefully she texted him back. *Thank you for everything.*

His response was immediate. *It's my pleasure. See you soon.*

Seremela checked her email messages and found a reply from Carling that the other woman must have sent even as Duncan drove to her apartment earlier. Of course Seremela could have as much time off as she needed, and she was to let Carling and Rune know if there was anything they could do to help.

Seremela had to smile. She didn't doubt for a minute that Carling had known very well what she was doing when she had shared Seremela's email with Duncan. Carling had already provided more help than Seremela could have hoped.

The weather changed drastically over the next hour, swirls of sunlit blue sky breaking through the ominous dark clouds. They would have to take care on route to the airport. Seremela had finished packing in plenty of time, and she had showered and changed for the trip into jeans and a sleeveless yellow, button-down cotton shirt.

She felt calm and optimistic by the time Duncan knocked on her door again—and then, of course, all of that went to hell. Her snakes spilled in a helter-skelter swirl around her shoulders. If they really had been dogs, she had no doubt they would have been barking and having a running fit.

Time to bite the bullet. She wasn't about to spend the next three or four days keeping the brats constantly under wrap under extreme desert heat, even though they totally deserved it. She squared her shoulders, marched over to the door and opened it.

"Hello, Seremela," said Duncan. "Have you had time to—?"

She caught one glimpse of him. He, too, had changed into an outfit very similar to hers, wearing jeans and a gray T-shirt that molded to his lean torso and muscled biceps. Previously whenever Seremela had seen him, he had always been the epitome of cool male elegance. It was shocking, somehow, to see him so casually dressed.

Or at least she thought it was. She didn't get a good enough look to be sure. Her snakes obscured her vision as they swarmed around her shoulders and over her head, shooting toward Duncan any way they could. The strength of their reaction surprised her and caught her off balance. She stumbled forward a step, which was all they needed.

Duncan began to laugh as her snakes wrapped around his neck and his upper arms. He caught her under her elbows as she stumbled, and they stood staring at each other, entwined. Something electric sparked in his eyes. She didn't know what it was, but the strength of it affected her powerfully. Her skin flashed with heat.

"I'm sorry," she mumbled. "It's only—you know they just like you, and—"

"Don't apologize," he told her in a gentle voice. He touched her cheek with the fingertips of one hand. "Like I've told you, I enjoy them."

Others might thrill to the crash and thunder of tumultuous passion. For Seremela, the most lethal thing in the world was exactly this kind of gentleness, this type of moment. They stood near enough to each other that she could see how his dark eyes had dilated, a subtle enough change in color that if she had stood even a few feet away, she wouldn't have caught it. He looked at her intently, his face sharpened with that same electric expression that pierced through his gaze, yet he touched her as lightly as snowflakes drifting down to rest on her sensitive skin.

She was intensely aware of each of the four small points of contact, even more so because she could barely feel them, and they held so steady, so steady, as he looked deep into her eyes. That single, innocent touch was almost unbelievably erotic. The steady light contact said things, and the very fact that he paused so long meant that he made sure she heard it.

It said his exquisite gentleness was no accident. It said he had to be intimately aware of the placement and position of her body to achieve such a delicate, butterfly touch. It said he touched her because he wanted to touch her, and that he knew how to be gentle and tender, that he was confident and didn't shy away from scrutiny, and that he could hold steady when he needed to.

It said he knew very well that she was clever enough to hear all of the nuances in his unspoken message.

Her breathing grew ragged. Her lips trembled as her snakes held him in position and he smiled into her eyes. And all he did was touch her cheek.

"Are you ready to go?" he said quietly, his fabulous, famous voice pitched for her ears alone.

And that was it, man, she just about came right there in her pants. The fact that she didn't was a miracle. She should be glad about it, since she could hope to maintain some semblance of dignity....

She glanced sideways at her snakes which had locked around him. One had wrapped around his biceps so far it was peering at her upside down, from underneath his arm.

Yeah well, she might not be able to maintain dignity exactly.

LET GO! she ordered. It was as stern a mental voice as she had ever used on them.

She must have startled them because they loosened and slipped back over her shoulders. Grateful, she took a deep breath and stepped back. She said aloud, somewhat hoarsely, "Yes, I'm ready."

He inclined his sleek, dark head with a smile, stepped inside and picked up her carry-on, while she looked around her apartment one last time, checked to make sure she had her iPhone, and shut and locked the door as they left.

Internally she was flipping rapidly through her Rolodex of teeming emotions. What to label this feeling? She had roared through embarrassment several minutes ago, so nah, that wasn't it. As they rode the elevator down to the garage in silence, she finally had to admit, she didn't know what she felt. She had never felt it before, so it wasn't in her Rolodex.

She did know the emotion held a large amount of shock and amazement.

Because *all he did was touch her cheek*.

And now all she could do was wonder, what else could he say in that silent, sensual language of his?

What poems could his fingers whisper as they danced across her skin?

What eloquent prose could he share with his body?

She had assumed they would be flying out of the Miami International Airport and was surprised when Duncan drove them instead toward Kendall-Tamiami Executive Airport, thirteen miles southwest of downtown Miami. Breaking the silence for the first time since they had left her apartment, she said, "I didn't know there were any commercial flights out of this airport."

He gave her a brief smile. "There aren't, but there are corporate flights. We're not taking a commercial flight. We're using the agency plane."

"Oh, I see."

The possibility hadn't even crossed her mind, and she was frankly staggered.

Rune and Carling had given her so much already. Carling had given her a papyrus sketch she had made in ancient Egypt, of a long-dead, half serpent, half human woman who, according to legend, had founded the medusa race. While the worth of the sketch didn't matter to Carling, the fact remained that it would still fetch a small fortune from a museum if Seremela ever chose to sell it. Then there was the new job, for which they paid her an extremely competitive salary, gave her a great benefit package and even paid for her relocation expenses. Now they gave her an unspecified amount of time off and were lending their agency plane.

When they returned, she would have to thank them properly, in person. The least she could do was have them over for supper. Carling could enjoy an excellent bottle of wine, and Rune certainly had a hearty enough appetite for several normal men combined.

Her gaze slid sideways to Duncan. Perhaps Duncan could join them. She smiled, feeling warm all over at the thought.

They parked, and Seremela glanced at the sky again as they exited the car. To the north, the sky had turned almost entirely blue. She could see the rays of sunshine spilling over the edge of dark clouds like laser beams. Her stomach tightened at the sight, and she turned to Duncan anxiously.

He glanced at the sky and gave her a calm smile. "It's all right. We've got a few more minutes. There's enough time to board."

"If you say so." She took her case as he handed it to her. Then he took his two cases, slammed the trunk and they strode toward the building. Once they were inside, she was able to take a deep breath again, but in order to board the Gulfstream jet, they had to go back outside again.

Duncan remained calm the entire time, and he never pulled out a cloak but he did take the stairway ramp to the plane at a lope just as sunshine spilled out over the northwestern border of the airport runway.

"Good gods," she muttered as he disappeared inside the plane. She glanced at the plane windows, noting that they were already lowered. His entire life was like this, a never-ending dance to avoid the sun. Feeling somewhat wrung out, she followed him at a slower pace up the ramp.

The pilot and her copilot were the plane's entire staff, and they greeted Duncan and Seremela cheerfully as they took their luggage to stow. Duncan held onto one piece of luggage long enough to pull out a laptop and a slim briefcase. He smiled at Seremela. "I hope you don't mind if I focus on work for a while."

"Of course not," she said. "This isn't a vacation. I would have brought work too, if I thought I could concentrate enough to get anything done. Well, that, and half my job involves growing nasty things in petri dishes."

He laughed. "Thank you for not bringing your work with you."

She grinned. "You're welcome."

The plane had a couch, and after takeoff when Duncan settled to work at a table, Seremela gave into temptation and stretched out to rest. Her sleepless night had caught up with her. The copilot brought her a pillow and a blanket and she curled on her side, her snakes spilling down her body and coiling in the natural hollow made by the indentation of her waist.

She dozed, rousing slightly every time she heard Duncan's voice. Mostly he was arranging for his time out of the office for the next several days, but once she surfaced to wakefulness with a pulse of alarm.

She clenched without moving, and she knew all of her snakes were awake and coiled with readiness too. The plane's engine ran strong and smoothly, and all seemed normal. What was it that had woken her?

Then she heard it again, Duncan speaking in a voice so cold and sharp it speared through the silence in the cabin like a stiletto. "…the fact remains, Julian, Carling's house is on an island in an Other land. Further, you can only access the passageway to the island from the ocean. Do you think she chose any of this by accident? It is not in the Nightkind demesne, so it does not fall under your legal domain. We have been patient now for a year."

Wow, he was really angry at this Julian guy. Then realization jangled through her. Duncan wasn't talking to just any Julian, but to Julian Regillus, the Nightkind King and Carling's estranged progeny.

Duncan paused, clearly listening to whatever was said on the other end of the line. Then he said icily, "That's unacceptable. Carling's magical library is too dangerous.

She doesn't trust anyone else to move it. She needs to move it herself, and you cannot continue to block her access to her own property." Another pause. "It's too late for that. She's done waiting. We've already filed a petition with the Elder tribunal. It's only a matter of time until the tribunal approves it."

Then another silence that stretched on, until she realized that Duncan wasn't pausing to listen but that the phone call had ended without goodbyes. Cautiously she peeked around the edge of the couch.

Anger etched the lines of Duncan's expression, turning him into a hard faced stranger. His dark eyes glittered, shards of black in his pale face. The gentle, urbane man she had become acquainted with and liked so well was nowhere to be seen, and what was left in his place was something entirely dangerous.

Then he caught sight of her peering around the arm of the couch, and the hardness in his expression eased.

She said, "I'm sorry. I overheard some of that."

He shook his head and sighed, running his hands through his hair until he actually looked rumpled. She frowned. Maybe that shouldn't seem as adorable to her as it did, especially after what she had just seen in his expression.

"No, it is I who should be apologizing—again—to you," he said. "I woke you, didn't I?"

She didn't bother to deny it but just regarded him steadily. "As soon as I realized who you were talking to, I should have done something to let you know I was awake, like gone to the lavatory."

Even though he didn't need to breathe, his humanity had not left him, she saw, as he blew out a breath. "You absolutely should not have done that," he said. "I didn't realize I would be transferred to Julian himself, or I never would have called. Then at that point the phone call took a dive straight into the toilet."

"Well, since the damage is done," she said, as she sat up. "If you don't mind me asking, why won't Julian let Carling have access to the island? Is it because he doesn't want her to have her library?"

"I don't think so," Duncan said. "It's useless as anything but a retreat. As an Other land, it's illegal for anyone from Earth to harvest anything from the island for commercial gain, and Carling has filed evidence that an intelligent indigenous winged species lives in the redwoods. And Julian doesn't give a damn one way or another about Carling's library. In fact, he insists that Carling send librarian witches to pack it all up and transport it. On the other hand, Carling insists—and she does have the legal right of it—that she have free access to her own house and that she sees to the transportation of the library personally."

"But he doesn't want to let her do that," she said.

"No, he doesn't," Duncan said. "Now that he's made his stance and exiled her, he doesn't want to allow Carling anywhere near the border of his demesne, especially at the crossover passageway for the island where it would be so easy for her to slip quietly into the Nightkind demesne. He certainly does not want to acknowledge that she has the right to come and go as she pleases."

She sat up and folded the blanket, and he slid out from the table where his work lay spread and walked over to sit beside her on the couch. Three of her snakes slipped over his shoulder to peer at him.

He smiled and held out his hand to them. They twined around his forearm as she confessed, "I always wondered how you felt about their estrangement."

"To be brutally fair, I can see both sides," he said. "Julian made some mistakes and trusted the wrong person, and last year Carling really had been dangerous to be around. I think they could actually get past it all if Julian was willing to submit to Carling's dominance again. But I also think something inside of him has broken, and he can't do that again. And I must take Carling's side in all of this."

The conversation had slipped squarely into Vampyre territory, and Seremela frowned, unsure about how comfortable she felt with the subject. She looked down at her hands as she said carefully, "The bond between a Vampyre maker and her progeny is something difficult to understand from the outside. I suppose you must take Carling's side, mustn't you?"

"Do you mean, did Carling order me to take her side?" Duncan asked. He smiled at her, all vestiges of the hard edged stranger gone. "No, she didn't. She wouldn't do that. I must take Carling's side because I love her, and I agree with her stance more than I agree with Julian's.

But that doesn't mean I can't see Julian's side of things too."

His ability to see all perspectives of a situation would be one of the things that made him such an outstanding attorney. She had to smile. It could make him an outstanding friend as well. Or enemy. It was one more thing that she liked so much about him. His quiet, incisive intelligence had its own kind of bite.

He was still speaking. He said, "And there's also a big difference between me and Julian."

"What difference is that?" she asked, growing fascinated despite her initial discomfort.

A thrill ran through her nerve endings as Duncan took one of her hands and played with her fingers. "Thousands of years," he told her. "You see, I accept Carling's rule over me. She made me, and I'm young enough to remember how I felt when I agreed to that. Yes, she has the Power to force me to her will, but in the last hundred and seventy years, she has almost never done so, and she never has without having a compelling reason for it. But Julian was turned at the height of the Roman Empire. He and Carling, and Rune too—the three of them are different from us."

"Us?" she repeated in surprise. "As in you and me?"

"Yes, as in you and me," he said.

She smiled at him, amused. "Do you realize I'm probably close to two hundred years older than you?"

He grinned. "I was thirty when I was turned, so if you're over three hundred and fifty, then yes, you are. But the age difference between you and me is a drop in the bucket when you look at millennia. They are all so much older than we are. I think it makes them fundamentally different in some way. And Julian is very dominant. Carling has never changed anyone against their will, so he must have once, long, long ago, agreed to her dominance, but I think he has chafed under her Power for a very long time. Imagine what it must have been like for him when it looked like she was dying."

She frowned. "I suppose, even if he cared for her, in some ways it must have felt like a relief."

"That is how I see it," Duncan said. "For many years they worked well in partnership with each other. They played off each other's strengths very well. But she didn't die when she was supposed to, and he wasn't freed. Now he can't stand the thought of being under her Power again. And if they ever saw each other in person, she could potentially force him to her will—he is her progeny, after all. I don't think Julian ever hated Carling before. But I think maybe he has learned to hate her now."

"The way you describe it, it sounds like they're in the middle of some kind of duel."

"That's a good way to describe it," Duncan said. "Only this duel may take centuries to play out."

She shuddered and curled her fingers around his. "It disturbs me to think about you possibly getting caught in the middle of their—" What should she call it? Disagreement sounded far too simple. "Their clash of wills."

"Oh well," he said wryly. "'Every family has its ups and downs.'"

Seremela went into delighted shock. "Did you just quote Katherine Hepburn as Eleanor of Aquitaine from *The Lion in Winter*, or was that an accident?"

He smiled into her gaze. "What if I did?"

Under the full bore force of such close contact, her breathing grew restricted. "I loved that movie."

"I did too. I've also had a lot of reason to quote it through recent years." He pressed a kiss against the back of her hand. "Speaking of families, I think we're getting ready to land. Once we get the SUV and our supplies, it should take us about an hour to get to Devil's Gate. Then we can collect your niece and take her home."

She chuckled. "You make it sound so easy."

"After Carling and Julian? You bet, this is easy," Duncan said.

Seremela shook her head at him and gave him a pitying grin. "You say that only because you haven't met Vetta yet."

Chapter Four

Death

B y the time the plane had landed at the Reno-Tahoe Airport and they had disembarked, met with the travel agency Duncan had used to book the SUV, signed for the vehicle and then inspected the food, water and camping supplies to make sure they had everything they needed, most of the daylight had slipped away. Duncan drove and once they reached US-395 S, traffic opened up and they made good time.

Reno was like many cities in the desert where they seemed to leave the populated area all at once. As he picked up speed on the open highway, he asked Seremela, "Do you mind if I roll down the windows?"

"Not at all," she said, although he noticed that she glanced at the western sky.

The sun hadn't completely set but it was low enough on the horizon that at times it was obscured by the hills in the west. The colors of the summer desert evening were large splashes of deepening tan and gold sliced with elongated black shadows, and the departing day left fiery banners of rose, lavender and purple strewn across the sky.

Duncan touched the controls embedded in the driver's seat door, and the windows lowered several inches. Nevada could reach triple digits in the heat of the day in June, but the heat cooled rapidly in the evening and the fresh air merely felt pleasantly warm.

After a moment, he said, "You know, some Vampyres are rigid about eschewing daylight hours. They will not step outside of shelter until the sun has completely set, and they are well under cover by sunrise every morning. It happens a lot with older Vampyres. Some of them turn agoraphobic and almost never leave their shelters. I'm not sure why. Perhaps as time goes by, they feel the odds stacking against them for having a fatal accident."

She stirred. A few of her snakes had lifted to the open window, tongues flickering to taste the desert air. To his amusement, a few others rested on his right shoulder. "I guess I can understand that," she said. "Sunlight is so lethal for you."

He nodded. "We live side-by-side with death. It's always there, just a few hours ahead or behind us, around the corner, or a few steps out from the shelter of a roof. But when Carling turned me, I told myself that I would not become like those other Vampyres. I would take sensible precautions but never live in fear."

"What kind of precautions do you take?" she asked.

"Well, for one thing, I do have a large house," he said. "If I have to take shelter from the sun, I refuse to feel cramped when I do. All the windows have metal shutters that operate on a timer. They automatically close and lock from sunrise to sundown." The system took a manual override code to open them any time during the day. Nobody was letting sunlight spear into Duncan's home without his express permission.

"I've heard of those shutters," she said. "Don't Carling and Rune have the same kind of thing in their new home too?"

"Yes." He slanted a glance at her. "And I can't tell you how exciting it was when full spectrum sunscreen became available. I would slather it all over and comb it through my hair before sunscreen spray made that a lot easier. For a while I looked like a throwback to a 1940s mafia kingpin."

She chuckled and relaxed. "So it really helps?"

"It does," he told her. "It protects against accidentally coming in contact with direct sunlight, and it can give a Vampyre up to ten minutes of leeway time to find shade. It has limitations—no Vampyre in his right mind would totally trust his life to waterproof sunscreen and go swimming in the daytime. But it's especially effective at dawn and dusk, like now, when any sunlight is indirect and fading fast. And I always wear it whenever I go out in the daytime."

"Good to know," she said. "I suppose you use sunscreen clothing too."

"Of course," he said. "All of my clothes are made of UPF 50+ material that blocks up to 98 percent of UV rays. On its own, it's not enough, but it is added insurance. And whenever I have to go out in the day, I always keep a cloak nearby, which is also made with sunscreen cloth."

As he gave her the information, he could see that her natural scientific curiosity had taken over and her nervousness eased. The silence that fell between them after that was thoughtful and companionable, and he smiled to himself.

He'd have to be a liar or blind to claim he wasn't affected by her beauty, because he was, but what really engaged his interest was her quick mind. It was such a goddamn pleasure to seduce an intelligent woman.

Because that's what he was going to do. Seduce her. Yeah, this lowdown dirty dog was going on the hunt. He would coax her into sharing her secrets of warmth and passion while candlelight gilded the insanely gorgeous iridescence of her skin. Just the thought of it made his fangs descend, and the whip of the night air turned exhilarative as his groin tightened painfully.

His urges and feelings were in an uproar every time he thought of her or let his imagination run unleashed. So much for compartmentalizing his appetites.

Maybe he would bite her.

Maybe she would bite him.

He kept his mouth shut and his jaw clenched, and he was savagely glad for the deep shadows in the car, and that somehow he managed to keep the vehicle steady on the road.

Maybe she would bite him all over.

Goddamn.

✧   ✧   ✧

Despite the fact that they had left the city behind and drove in full desert, traffic picked up again when he turned onto State Road 342. Soon a glow of light shone like a dome against the darkness of the night sky, and Duncan knew they were getting close. He followed the flow of vehicles which slowed to a crawl on the two-lane highway, until they came upon a shadowed wall of rock that rose on either side of the road.

"There it is," Seremela whispered.

An elusive tingle of land magic brushed his senses, along with a sense of other magic sparks flaring in the distance.

Their headlights flashed on a historical marker. Duncan caught a glimpse of the text but it was too small and dense to read. Several yards past the marker, a large, clapboard sign had been erected. Written in orange neon spray paint, the words jumped off the board.

The sign read:

Devil's Gate

Pop: ~~28, 993 suckas~~

~~69,345~~

Past ~~100,000~~

Who the fuck knows?

He glanced at Seremela who looked back at him, wide-eyed. Then they both burst out laughing. Seremela said, "Even if the tent city is outlandishly bloated, medusae are rare enough that it won't be hard to find her. People tend to take notice when we are around."

"I'm sure they do," Duncan said. Giving in to impulse, he trailed his fingers down her warm, slender forearm and clasped her hand. Her breath caught, the tiny sound all but inaudible, but with his sharp Vampyre's hearing, he heard it easily.

She didn't pull away. Instead she turned her hand over and held his, palm to palm. He rubbed his thumb along the smooth skin on the back of her hand and wondered how she could sit there so calmly, because good gods, he was on fire all over for her, and she seemed completely unaware of the fact. He knew he had a good courtroom face, but he didn't know it was that good.

He drove one-handed, staying sedately in a line that crept toward the tent city at ten miles an hour. A few trucks pulled away and drove off over open land, but without knowing the terrain, he judged it best to follow the main stream of vehicles for now.

They were being stopped up ahead by a hulking troll who then directed them toward the right where they parked in a line. When it came his turn, Duncan released Seremela's hand and rolled his window down further.

The SUV creaked as the troll laid a hand on the roof and bent down to peer inside at them with small eyes and an incurious expression on his gray rock-like face. "Parking in our lot is three hundred a night," the troll rumbled. "Cash only."

Duncan's eyebrows raised. "Their lot." If any of them actually owned this piece of land, he was Pee-wee Herman.

"Three hundred dollars!" Seremela exclaimed, leaning forward. "A night?"

The troll gave her an indifferent glance. "You want to keep your car from being stolen? You want to keep your stuff, and all your tires too? That'll be three hundred dollars. In advance. You don't like it, lady, go park somewhere else, and good fucking luck with that, 'cause you're gonna need it."

For three hundred dollars a night, Duncan could get a room at one of the best hotels in San Francisco, one of the most expensive cities in the world. He shook his head and shifted in his seat to pull out his wallet.

"Duncan!" Seremela exclaimed telepathically. *"That's highway robbery."*

"Of course it is," he said. *"The troll and his organization probably vandalize and steal from anyone who doesn't use their parking lot. But if it keeps our supplies untouched and we can get away trouble free, it will be worth it."*

He pulled cash out of his wallet and offered it to the troll. The massive fingers closed over one end of the bills and tugged, but Duncan held on to them until the troll looked at him in exasperation. He said softly, "Anything happens, and I'm holding you personally responsible. Not anybody else. You, bucko."

Maybe the troll finally took a good look at his face and recognized him. Trolls were Nightkind creatures too, and Duncan was, after all, extremely well known. Or maybe something in Duncan's voice got to him. Whatever it was, the troll masticated his massive jaw as if he chewed on something sour, but he muttered, "Nuthin's gonna happen."

"Very good," Duncan said. He let go of the cash and flicked two twenty dollar bills out of his wallet. "After we park, we're going to need reliable information. Where?"

"Down Main Street, north side," said the troll. "Look for the pharmacist. Name's Wendell. He'd sell pics of his mother's tits to the highest bidder. But they'd really be of his mother's tits." As Seremela stared, the troll lifted his rocky shoulders. "What can I say, guy's got a code. Sort of."

Duncan bit back a smile. "He your boss?"

"Yeah." The troll patted the roof of the SUV, straightened and lumbered back a step. "Now git outta here."

Duncan drove the SUV gently over the rough, pitted ground toward the end of one row of vehicles where a ghoul in an orange reflective vest stood, flashing them with a flashlight.

"I brought cash too," Seremela said. "I'll pay you back."

"Let's not worry about that right now," Duncan said. "It's unimportant. Let's just focus on getting your niece."

"Okay." She stayed silent for a moment as he parked the SUV. Then she said, "Wendell."

"The pornographer pharmacist," Duncan said, deadpan.

"It's not funny."

"Of course it's not," he said.

A soft, odd noise escaped her. It sounded a lot like hot air hissing out of a tea kettle. He looked at her suffused face, found her looking back at him, and then they both burst out laughing again.

He pulled the emergency brake and killed the engine. "Let's go see what Wendell has to say for himself."

"Okay," Seremela said, eyes dancing, "but if he tries to sell me a picture of his mother's tits, I'm so out of there."

Duncan laughed again. "Trust me, I'll be right on your heels."

They both sobered as they climbed out of the SUV. Duncan said, "The troll spoke the truth, but we should both keep a light pack with us just in case. This would not be a kind place to be stranded in without resources."

She nodded, her expression turning grim. She had a large soft bag with a shoulder strap, and she rifled through the contents and shifted over a few items from her carry-on. The last thing she added was a bottle of water. Then she pulled the shoulder strap over her head, lifted her snakes out of the way and settled it firmly across her torso.

Duncan's bag of essentials, with the weapons, money and sun protections, was a leather backpack. He pulled out a Beretta 9mm and a five inch hunting knife on a belt. After strapping the pack to his back, he buckled on the knife belt and tucked the gun into the waist of his jeans, making sure the butt was well visible.

Seremela's gaze lingered at his waist when he turned to her, but she said nothing about the weapons. She did not carry an obvious weapon, but he noticed that she did not tie back her snakes. Usually she bound them back loosely with a simple scarf at the base of her neck, as though they were dreadlocks. That allowed them to move around but limited their range of reach. Without them restricted in any way, she looked wilder, more feral and exceedingly deadly.

He heartily approved. He asked, "Okay?"

She nodded again. Face calm, eyes sharp. Gods, this woman was hotter than Death Valley in July.

He couldn't resist touching her again. He cupped her cheek and rubbed his thumb gently along the soft, plush arc of her lips. Her expression softened, and the look she gave him was filled with equal parts tenderness and amazement. He wanted to ask her what caused her to look so surprised when he touched her with affection. He wanted to kiss her slowly and savor that first, intimate taste of her.

Hunger hissed along his nerve endings and turned aggressive. Her mouth would be so soft, the tender flesh giving way under his. He wanted to coax her lips apart and enter her with his tongue, and just the thought of deepening the kiss was so sexual his groin tightened.

Someone shouted nearby, splintering the moment. Frowning, he glanced around at the dust filled parking lot then he offered Seremela his hand. She took it.

"After this is over and we get back to Miami," he asked, "where are we going to go for our first date?"

Half a dozen of her snakes rose up to stare at him, and the nictating membranes snapped shut over Seremela's eyes. Then opened. Then shut. And opened. She blinked rapidly and it stopped. "First date?"

He wondered what that meant. Perhaps she got sand in her eyes. He asked, "Will you go out with me when we get back? I like the opera. But I like rock concerts too, and I'm a sucker for a good movie."

Her delighted smile was truly one of the loveliest expressions he had ever seen on her face. "Yes," she said. "I like all of that too, but I especially like the opera."

"Perfect," he said with satisfaction. "It'll give us something to look forward to."

At the time, he had no idea how much that would matter.

Hand-in-hand, together they walked into Devil's Gate.

It was everything he had expected, and more: dirty, stinky, unpredictable and overcrowded. The night was windless, and smoke from campfires hung in the air, thick with the scent of cigarette smoke, cooking meat and onions.

The scene threw him into a cascade of memories. He remembered how incredulous he felt when he found out that his legal work had come to Carling's attention. She had still been Queen of the Nightkind then, and she courted him with the wily patience of a professional politician and all the wisdom of a seasoned courtesan, until they had reached an agreement, about business and about other things.

His last meal before she changed him had been a sixteen ounce porterhouse steak, medium rare, with fried potatoes, apple pie and cheddar cheese, and a Guinness.

He remembered each detail as if it were yesterday. The meat had been so juicy and tender, he could cut it with his fork, and the potatoes had been crisp, salty with butter and a rich golden brown. The apple pie had been both tart and sweet, the tang of the sharp cheddar its perfect complement, and damn, that Guinness had been frothy and yeasty, like a satisfying novel for the taste buds, telling its dark, full-bodied and soul-nourishing story with every swallow. He had eaten until he thought he would burst.

Even though he still dreamed about that meal, the real thing would turn his stomach now, and while the present day camp brought back vivid memories, there were plenty of differences too.

The hellish red glows from the flames were interspersed with the cold, thin illumination from LED camping lanterns. Different kinds of music clashed, most of it blaring from boom boxes, but the sound of a few instruments, a guitar, a fiddle and drums, carried the piercing, startling sweetness of live passion.

Painted prostitutes, both men and women, walked the "streets" between the tents, campers and a few mobile office buildings. Humans, Elves and Light Fae, Demonkind and Wyr, and of course, the Nightkind were out in force. Vampyres prowled the area, smiling white smiles, drawn by the lawlessness and the lure of so much living blood packed into one space. Duncan backed them off silently with a glittering look. The Vampyres took one look at his hard face and melted into the crowd.

The tent city was a melting pot with the burner turned on high. At any minute he expected a fight to break out, and he wasn't disappointed.

They had to sidestep two brawls as they navigated to "main street," the largest pathway that lay between camps.

He didn't pretend to himself that he was the only reason they remained unmolested. People took one look at Seremela, with her set expression, sharp gaze and snakes raised and wary, and they gave both of them a wide berth. When a drunk stumbled into her path and startled her, all her snakes whipped around and hissed at him, scaring him so badly he pissed himself as he ran away.

Duncan murmured to Seremela, "The California Gold Rush was so much more charming than this. I'm sure it was."

She glanced at him sardonically. "And I'm sure you have swamp land in Florida you'd like to sell me."

He grinned and said to a tired looking, sunburned human, "We're looking for the pharmacy. Do you know where it is?"

The human's gaze passed over him and lingered on Seremela. "Five or six camps down," she said. "It's one of the fancy ones. Hard to miss."

"Thanks."

"Wonder what she means by fancy," Seremela muttered.

They discovered the answer to that soon enough as they found one of the few mobile buildings several campsites down. A simple sign that said "Wendell's" hung outside the door. The pale, cold light of LED lamps glowed through the window, and the door was propped open to the night air. Wendell's was open for business.

Normally Duncan always invited a lady to go first through the door, but normal wasn't a definition that applied to this place. He stepped in first and looked around quickly, one hand on his gun. Inside, the mobile building was crowded with metal shelves filled with merchandise, anything from canned goods, tampons, toothpaste, aspirin and other pain relievers, and first aid supplies to other, more potent supplies.

Duncan's sharp glance took in the bottles of Oxy-Contin, Percocet and Demerol in a glass, locked cabinet behind a counter. He had no doubt that the right price, not a prescription, would be the key that would open up that cabinet. It also had a shelf of baggies filled with marijuana, some rolled and some loose, and a couple of shelves filled with dark brown tincture bottles, homeopathic concoctions that glinted with sparks of magic.

There were other people in the building. A few were obviously shoppers who took one look at Duncan and Seremela and then slipped out the open door. Duncan kept track of them until the last had left, but the main part of his attention was focused on the two people behind the counter.

One of them was a tall, dangerous looking Light Fae male, his curly blond hair shaved close to his skull, which made his pointed ears seem even longer. He wore two shoulder gun holsters over a tank top that bared a lot of golden brown skin. He watched Seremela with a flat, unfriendly gaze, resting a hand on one of his guns.

Duncan's jaw tightened. He did not like the sight of that. He turned his attention to the other person behind the counter, a short, slight human male with sharp eyes and a rather plain, aesthetic face. The male was easily the most intelligent person Duncan had laid eyes on since they arrived.

He said, "You must be Wendell."

"You're a quick one," said Wendell. "Hence the sign outside my door." He opened the foil wrap on a piece of Nicorette gum and popped it in his mouth, while his gaze took in everything about Duncan in one glance. "I recognize you. I know who you are." He turned and dissected Seremela appearance.

"You got here just in time for the execution, but I'm afraid bringing a lawyer even as famous as he is won't do you any good."

Everything inside Duncan went cold and quiet when the other man said execution.

Seremela looked at the pharmacist blankly. "Excuse me?"

Wendell's thin eyebrows rose. "You're here about the Tarot reader, aren't you? The one who offed Thruvial."

If anything, Seremela looked even more confused and disturbed. "I have no idea what you're talking about."

"Eh, my mistake," Wendell said, shrugging. "I thought since you were a medusa that was why you were here. Guess I'm as guilty of racial profiling as anybody else."

Duncan took a step forward, and the Light Fae muscle matched him step for step. He ignored the other male and said to the pharmacist, "Do you know how many medusae are here in Devil's Gate?"

Wendell scratched the back of his neck. "Aside from your companion, there's only one that I know of—the Tarot reader. Young girl maybe twenty years old, wears Goth makeup, got a mouth on her."

"Goth makeup? Oh gods, Duncan," Seremela said, her creamy skin going chalky. "He's talking about Vetta."

Fuck. *Fuck.*

"Yeah, that's her name," said Wendell. His sharp gaze had turned curious and more than a little avid. "I'll give you this much information for free, since it's common knowledge anyway. They say she poisoned a man a couple days ago. Someone who was very important here. They're going to hang her at dawn."

Chapter Five
The Depths

P anic and disorientation sank claws into Seremela and wouldn't let her go. Vetta was to be hanged? For poisoning someone?

She couldn't drag in a deep enough breath and struggled for air as she stared at the human and his Light Fae bodyguard.

The Light Fae bruiser stared back at her, his cynical expression turning wary. He took a couple steps back and drew his gun.

"Leash your dog," Duncan said sharply. "He's about to get stupid."

What dog? Duncan moved so fast he blurred, crowding her back against a wall. Seremela stared at him blankly. What the hell was he doing?

When he stopped, he stood between her and the Light Fae, and belated understanding slammed into her—he was shielding her with his body.

At the same moment the nerdy human snapped, "Holster it, Dain."

Lean, strong fingers came under her chin, and Duncan forcibly turned her face toward him. "Don't look at him," Duncan said to her in a quiet voice. "Look at me."

She tried to focus on him. That was when she realized all her snakes were hissing at the Light Fae. Her panic had turned them deadly. She could feel them, roused and wanting to bite, and as she looked over Duncan's shoulder, she could tell that the Light Fae male knew it.

"At me, Seremela," Duncan whispered gently.

Her attention shifted back to him. He raised a hand and stroked it along a few of the snakes, and they quit hissing and wrapped around his forearm.

Even though his back was turned to an unknown male with his gun drawn, Duncan looked calm, his dark gaze steady.

As soon as he knew he had gotten her attention, he smiled at her. *"They're not going to hang her,"* he said telepathically. *"We won't let them."*

She calmed, marginally. They were only two people in an overcrowded, dangerous and unknown place. Maybe it was ridiculous to believe him. Certainly it was neither sensible nor logical, but she did.

Impulsively she reached up to touch his lean cheek, more of the snakes reaching for him, and his gaze warmed. *"Duncan, I don't know what he's talking about,"* she said. *"Vetta isn't a Tarot reader, and she might be a total contrary shit, but she's not a murderer. That's insane. If—if by any chance she did kill someone, she wouldn't have had any other choice."*

He frowned. *"We need to ask some questions now. Whatever he says, we're going to make this right. Okay?"*

She nodded jerkily. *"Okay."*

He took her hand and kissed her fingertips, then carefully disengaged himself. Only then did he turn around to face the pharmacist and his Light Fae guard, who had holstered his gun.

All of her snakes had calmed as she had calmed. She gathered them to her and nudged them behind her shoulder as Duncan said, pleasantly, "Let's start this conversation over, shall we?"

Wendell regarded them both with narrowed eyes. "Fine, but you're scaring away my paying customers, so your free sample is over," he said, chewing gum. "You want to know anything else, you gotta pay. Standard 411 rate is ten dollars a minute, not including additional rates for premium intel."

Anger sparked in Seremela at the human's callousness. She had never in her life wanted to hurt another creature, but she was pretty sure she could hurt this one. *Just one bite,* she thought as she fixed a cold, level gaze on him. *All it would take is one, and your heart rate would slow, your skin would turn dry and flake off and you would be scared, nauseated and fucking miserable for a week. And I think I would like that very much.*

Even as she thought it, a single snake slipped over her shoulder and rose to the level of her cheekbone. It too stared at Wendell unblinkingly, until the human shifted on his stool and looked away.

Aw, she'd made him squirm. Yee-fucking-haw.

Duncan slipped his hands in his jeans pockets, standing relaxed. "Your rate's unimaginative but doable," he said.

The human's thin mouth tilted sourly, and he shifted again. "What the fuck do you mean by that?"

"There are much more valuable things than cash, Wendell," Duncan said. "Like alliances, protection and immunity."

Wendell's eyebrows rose. "You think you could offer me protection or immunity? You've barely set foot in this place. You have no social equity here, Vampyre. You don't know the Power brokers, and you have no alliances. You know nothing."

"The world is a much wider place than this dusty little pile of tents," Duncan said. He gave the human a cold smile, and a touch of a whip entered his voice, precisely balanced just so with a delicate lash of contempt. "But no worries, Wendell. If you want money, you'll get money. Tell us what happened, with details, names and times."

Wendell paused, regarding Duncan with equal parts greed and caution, and Seremela could tell he was rethinking the last few minutes. Then the pharmacist said, "There may not be any law here, but there is a balance of Power. Or there was, until one of the Power brokers was killed yesterday. Things are a bit destabilized at the moment."

"Who were the Power brokers, and what did they control?" Duncan asked. "You're not one of them."

"Nah," said Wendell as he glanced at his watch. "My motive is profit, not power. I'm strictly in parking and pharmaceuticals, with a side interest now and then in information. The real Power brokers in Devil's Gate are hard core. There's an Elf with an affinity to Earth. Caerlovena is her name. She's got a lock on most of the diggers. Then there's a Djinn, Malphas, who has a lock on all the casinos, and I mean all of them. And until yesterday, there was Cieran Thruvial, who locked on prostitutes and protection. All the shops and vendors owed him a cut of their take."

"Cieran Thruvial," Duncan said. Surprise flickered in his gaze. "I know that name."

Seremela shook her head. Inside she was reeling again. "That can't be right," she said. "I don't see Vetta turning to prostitution. I guess she could have, but I just don't see it."

Wendell shrugged. "Well, the girl read Tarot, or at least that's what her tent sign said. She charged for quarter hour and half hour readings. She did a good business too, from what I heard. I don't know if she was turning tricks on the side or not, but like a lot of other shop keepers, she owed Thruvial protection money. They had a tempestuous relationship and argued a lot in public. I gotta say, it seemed real intimate."

"Where is she now?" Seremela asked, the words scraping in her dry, constricted throat.

"Malphas is holding her until dawn," Wendell said, and for the first time since they met him, something like sympathy crept into his gaze. "Scary dude, that Djinn. I'm not sure what he cares about, if anything."

"Thruvial is a Fae name," Duncan said abruptly. "Was this Cieran Thruvial Dark Fae?"

This time, both Wendell and his guard shifted their attention to Duncan, their expressions sharpening. Speaking for the first time, the guard said, "Yes."

Wendell asked, "You knew him?"

Duncan's face had turned expressionless. He said, "I met him once."

"Where?" The pharmacist looked avid again.

Duncan gave him a sardonic smile. "That's not part of our agreement, Wendell. Where's the best place to find Malphas?"

Wendell made a face but said, "Much as he hangs anywhere, I guess it would be Gehenna—that's the name of his main casino. Get it? Devil's Gate—Gehenna. Ar ar ar, right?"

Duncan's dark gaze shifted to her. He asked the pharmacist, "What do we owe you?"

"You're not going to ask me how to find Gehenna?" Wendell asked.

Duncan shook his head. "We don't need you anymore."

"If I were you, I wouldn't be so quick to say that," Wendell said. "With Thruvial dead, things are shifting. People are making a grab for his territory, and a couple of them are strong magic users. You don't know who to watch out for, or where to go. You still don't know anything."

"Now you're trying too hard," Duncan told him. He pulled out some cash and laid it on the counter. "I make it just under fifteen minutes. Keep the change." He turned to Seremela, his expression softening. "Let's go."

She nodded and stepped out of the door, and he followed.

Wendell called after them, "You're making a mistake if you think you don't need me."

Duncan shook his head. Once they were outside, he offered Seremela his hand. She took it. His grip was like the rest of him, steady, calm and cool. She gripped it tightly and took a deep breath. The smoke scented night air seemed so much fresher than it had before they had stepped into Wendell's shop.

"What a scurvy little bug," she said between her teeth.

"I know. I want to squash him."

He pulled her around to face him, cupping her elbows in the palms of his hands while he watched the crowd behind her. After a quick glance at his face, she did the same, watching what happened at his back. The red-tinged light from various campfires was indirect. Nearby someone laughed, a sharp sound abruptly cut off. Magic tinged the air, mingling with the physical smells of spilt whiskey and other sour odors.

Would you leave if I asked you to?" he asked telepathically.

She glanced at his shadowed face quickly. He looked as casual and indifferent as if they were talking about the weather. A few choice responses occurred to her, but she saw too many reasons for why he asked what he did.

In the end she just simply said, *"No."*

He didn't look surprised. He nodded and rubbed his thumbs along the sensitive skin at the inside of her elbows, but she didn't think he was aware of what he was doing.

"The thing that bothers me is the Djinn," he said and frowned. *"Well, there's more than a few things that bother me."*

"Who was Thruvial?" she asked.

He met her gaze. *"Do you remember that I traveled last year with Carling to Adriyel for Niniane Lorelle's coronation?"*

"Yes," she said.

She wasn't likely to forget it.

Adriyel was the Dark Fae Other land, and last year had been eventful for the Dark Fae demesne. Dragos, the Lord of the Wyr, had killed Urien, the Dark Fae King, when Urien kidnapped Dragos's mate. Then the heir to the throne, Niniane Lorelle, who had been living under Dragos's protection, had to travel to Adriyel to claim her birthright. Along the way, Niniane had survived two assassination attempts in Chicago. Seremela had been the medical examiner who conducted an autopsy on the bodies of the would-be assassins.

The Wyr sentinel warlord Tiago had left his position in the Wyr demesne in New York to travel with Niniane and protect her. As far as the public knew, he now worked for the new Queen as her chief of security, but privately, those who knew the couple also knew that he had mated with Niniane.

Since that time, news from Adriyel had come out in snippets interspersed with weeks of silence. A few months after her coronation, the new Dark Fae Queen had imprisoned several noblemen and tried them for crimes committed against the crown, including treason, conspiracy, the regicide of her father and the murders of the rest of her family. Shortly after the trials, the conspirators had been executed.

A short time after, around January or so, Adriyel had officially opened its borders to tourism and open trade. Still, six months later, it was rare to see Dark Fae in the general public.

Seremela asked, *"Did you meet Thruvial in Adriyel?"*

"Yes, briefly," Duncan said. *"Thruvial was a nobleman, and I was just a part of Carling's entourage, so he and I had no reason to strike up a conversation. But I have a good memory for names and faces, and I remember him at the coronation and the celebration afterwards. Why would he come here, of all places?"*

Now he had her frowning as well. Urgency pounded in her veins. She needed to get to her niece. Vetta had finally bitten off more than she could chew, and the poor little shit had to be scared out of her mind. Sometimes people had to hit rock bottom before they could change. If that was true, Seremela didn't think there was any lower Vetta could go than sitting in the dark tonight, all alone, while she waited for her own execution.

But as much as Seremela wanted to barge over to Gehenna, Duncan was right to pause and assess the situation. They needed clear heads and to understand as much as they could about what was really going on, and part of that meant trying to understand the victim and why he had been killed.

She said, "*The Dark Fae are famous for their metallurgy. Maybe the possibility of finding a node of magic-rich metal lured him here, especially now that trade has opened up between Adriyel and the rest of the world.*"

"*Maybe, but if that was the case,*" Duncan said, "*why didn't Thruvial send servants or employees? Why come himself? And once he got here, why did he get involved in trafficking, and not excavation and mining?*"

"*I don't know,*" she said, as frustration welled up.

His grip tightened. He repeated, "*But what really bothers me is the Djinn's presence here, and his involvement. Seremela, if you left, you could reach Reno inside an hour. You could call out until you get cell phone reception, talk to Carling and Rune and tell them what is going on while I go talk to this Malphas and see what I can do here.*"

"*I'm not leaving,*" she told him.

He looked as disturbed as she had ever seen him, and even a little angry. "*I don't want you to stay here.*"

He was that worried about her?

She said gently, "*Duncan, think for a moment. It would be nice if one of us could leave and tell the outside world what is going on, but there* is *a Djinn involved, and information works both ways. What if Wendell decides that other people would be willing to pay for what he learned about us? What if one of them is the Djinn? Nobody here has any legal authority or any right to execute Vetta. Hanging her is* murder. *I could get halfway to Reno— hell, we could both leave and he could still stop us if he wanted to.*" She paused to let that point sink in. "*We couldn't know it at the time, but we hit the point of no return the moment we stepped into Wendell's shop. We need to confront whatever this is together, head on. Right now."*

"Gods damn it," he whispered. His lips pulled back from his teeth where, she saw, a hint of his fangs showed. Then his grip on her elbows loosened, and he stroked his fingers lightly down her forearms before he let her go. "All right. Let's find Gehenna."

The casino was easy to locate. It sat at the edge of the settlement in a large circus-sized tent. Raucous noise poured out of it, and drunks milled about the opening. Inside a blaze of electric lights flashed atop rows of slot machines. Malphas, or his casino managers, had invested in importing electric generators. Cigarette, cigar and hashish smoke hazed the air.

Seremela caught sight of movement out of the periphery of her vision and looked up. A boardwalk had been constructed around the edge of the tent where several large Goblins, weapons prominently displayed, walked and watched the crowd below.

Her lip curled. She and Duncan exchanged a glance then moved further into the tent where they found the game tables. People caught sight of Seremela and moved to give them both a wide berth.

She was okay with that. She wanted a three foot space between her and anyone else in this hellhole.

Male and female servers, both Elder Races and human, carried drinks and trays of chips for people to buy, dressed only in waist chains and dog collars. While

Seremela wasn't a prude by any means, she didn't like strangers' dangly bits paraded in front of her without warning, and she jerked her gaze away with a muttered curse.

A human server approached them with a bright smile, although Seremela noted that he came up on Duncan's far side, staying well away from her.

"Want to buy some chips?"

"We want a manager," Duncan said.

His smile never faltering, the server said, "Yeah, good luck with that. It's a busy night, but they're all real busy. Days too. Gehenna never closes, no matter how hot it gets. Offices are straight ahead."

"Thanks," Duncan said.

They barely took three steps forward when a female Vampyre, flanked by two Goblins, shouldered through the crowd toward them. The Vampyre had short blonde hair and was dressed in black fatigue pants and a black tank top, which showed off her muscled torso. She wore a semiautomatic in a hip holster and she moved like a fighter. She also looked intelligent, and she stopped right in front of them.

After one comprehensive glance at Duncan, the Vampyre focused on Seremela. "If you want to stay in Gehenna, you have to wrap up your snakes. You're disturbing the customers."

"We're not here to gamble and we have no intention of staying on the floor," Seremela said quietly. "We're here to talk to Malphas."

The Vampyre rubbed the back of her neck and studied them both under leveled brows. "You're here about the girl, aren't you?" she said. When neither of them confirmed nor denied, she shook her head. "Follow me."

Dismissing the two Goblins, the Vampyre led them through the crowd to the back of the tent. Then, without stopping, she led them outside through another opening. Behind the tent several modular buildings had been set up, the area surrounded by a nine foot high barbed wire fence. Seremela looked around everywhere as they walked. She knew in her bones that Vetta was very close, probably in one of these buildings.

"She's here," Seremela said to Duncan. *"I know she is."*

He moved as calmly as ever, hands loose at his sides, but she noticed how his sharp gaze roamed over the scene. *"I believe you,"* he said. *"I think she's here too."*

Their Vampyre escort was apparently not much for idle chitchat, for she didn't say a word until they reached the last modular building. Once there, she propped open the door and flipped on an inside light. Duncan looked in but didn't step inside. Seremela glanced in too. The interior was totally empty and lit by a single naked light bulb.

The Vampyre said, "If you want to talk to Malphas, go in and call him. He'll come or not, as it suits him. If you've changed your mind, leave. Either way, the hanging is at dawn."

Seremela clenched her fists and started after the Vampyre, snakes hissing. She ran into a barrier as Duncan's arm shot out to block her way. "Easy, darling," he said quietly to her. Telepathically, he said, *"Don't waste your energy on her. She doesn't matter. We've got more important things to focus on."*

She sucked in a breath and struggled to rein in her temper. He was right. This Vampyre didn't matter in the slightest. She gave him a curt nod, and he dropped his arm and stepped inside. With one last glare at the Vampyre, Seremela followed.

Inside the building was just as bare and unadorned as her first glance had told her it was. Metal walls, metal floor, metal ceiling. No chairs, no carpet, no wall hangings or desks.

After they had both turned in a circle, Duncan shrugged at her and said into the apparent emptiness, "Malphas."

At first nothing happened, and a raging despair threatened to take Seremela over. He had to come. He had to.

Then black smoke slid into the building through the open door, and the air began to compress. Power built and built. It pressed against them so that Seremela's breathing felt constricted and she had to swallow hard. This was a very old one, possibly a first generation Djinn. What was a first generation Djinn doing at Devil's Gate?

The Power coalesced into the form of a tall, golden haired man, with an angelically beautiful face and two supernovas for eyes. Those piercing twin stars fixed on them, and the beautiful man gave them a deadly smile.

Malphas said, "Welcome to Gehenna."

Chapter Six

Love

"What can I do for you?" the Djinn asked. Danger breathed along the back of Duncan's neck. After one glance at him, Malphas turned to Seremela, who regarded him with a calm yet tense expression. Her snakes draped across her arms and shoulders, and all of them watched the Djinn too.

"We were told my niece is going to be executed for murder at dawn," Seremela said. "It isn't true. Vetta would not commit murder."

"Ah," said Malphas as he gestured with one long white hand. "I'm afraid that the truth has limited efficacy, especially here."

With that one simple sentence, the danger in the room skyrocketed.

No honorable Djinn that Duncan had ever met or heard of would have said such a thing, because the Djinn prized truth along with all other forms of information.

"Be careful," Duncan said to Seremela. She gave him a startled glance as he asked, "Which House are you with, Malphas?"

The Djinn considered him for a moment. Then Malphas chuckled. "You believe the answer to this has any relevance?"

"With the Djinn," Duncan said in a polite tone of voice, "the answer to this is always relevant."

Malphas inclined his head in acknowledgment. "I hail from the House Shaytan."

"Currently?" Duncan asked.

Malphas's smile widened. "No."

"Duncan, what's going on?" Seremela's telepathic voice sounded tense.

He kept his attention fixed on the deadly creature in front of him, the muscles in his body clenching tight. *"He's a pariah, Seremela. A very Powerful one."*

"I don't know much about Djinn society," she said. Her expression turned fearful as she picked up on his wariness. *"I don't know what that means."*

"I do," he told her grimly.

The five Djinn Houses were built on their associations, and their associations were built on their word. A Djinn who broke his word was perceived as having no honor by other Djinn, and he became a pariah, without association with any of the Houses, lawless and rogue.

Seremela had said they had hit the point of no return when they stepped into Wendell's shop, but here at Gehenna they had stepped into a place that was far worse, and infinitely more dangerous.

Scary dude, Wendell had said about the Djinn. *I'm not sure what he cares about.*

A stiletto of cold, icy certainty sliced through Duncan.

Whatever Malphas cared about, it wasn't the truth, or the law. As a first generation Djinn, he would have the Power to know whether or not Vetta was telling the truth if she claimed she was innocent. Since he was still holding her in custody, he didn't care who had actually killed Thruvial. Hanging Vetta must benefit him in some way, only now Duncan and Seremela had shown up to protest.

Malphas hadn't come to this empty trailer to talk with them. He had come to figure out whether or not he should kill them too. The only reason why Duncan and Seremela were still alive was because the Djinn had not yet decided what course of action was in his best interest.

"Things were different when the girl was a nobody, weren't they?" Duncan said. Malphas strolled leisurely around him, and he turned to keep the Djinn in front of him. "Because then nobody cared if she died. What I don't understand is why hang her in the first place?"

"She's a stupid child," Malphas said. His tone was casually dismissive, as if they talked about a disobedient dog. "She's insolent and rude, and she has behaved as though everybody else owes her something. Before you arrived, there was no one here in Devil's Gate to miss her and several people who would say good riddance. In the meantime someone of Power—someone who had taken hold of a great deal of power here—has been killed, and there are many other Powerful creatures present who are disturbed by that. They want retribution.

They want to know that the same thing cannot happen to them and go unpunished. They hear the word 'poison,' they see a medusa—" The Djinn let the sentence trail away as he shrugged. "The clamor to hang her became too loud to ignore. She had to be held somewhere, so I took her."

"Then give us a chance to find out who really killed him," Seremela said. Her eyes burned with repressed emotion but, Duncan was glad to see, her face and voice remained calm. "I'm—I've been a medical examiner. If I could examine the body, I can determine what type of poison was used and possibly learn a great deal more. I can guarantee you this much—even if Vetta's snakes bit him repeatedly, they're much too immature to carry enough poison to kill a mature Dark Fae male."

"Keep a poisoned, rotting corpse here, in this heat?" said Malphas, his beautiful face twisting with distaste. "Oh no, Doctor. While your offer might carry a certain theoretical merit, there is no body left for you to examine."

"What do you mean, there's no body?" Seremela asked tightly. "What happened to it?"

"Thruvial's own attendants lacked the proper Dark Fae herbs for preserving the dead. His remains turned so foul they were forced to burn him on a pyre yesterday."

As Duncan listened, his mind raced. Discovering what the Djinn cared about was the key that would get them out of this trailer alive.

The Djinn didn't care who killed Thruvial, and he didn't especially care one way or another about using

Vetta for a scapegoat, or he would have hanged her when Thruvial's murder had first been discovered.

Why had the Djinn gotten involved in the first place? What did he gain from it?

Then Duncan had it, what Malphas cared about.

Earlier Wendell the pharmacist had even coined the term. Malphas owed his life to balancing power. As a first generation Djinn who was also a pariah, he lived with the constant risk of being hunted by others of his kind.

For the other Djinn, however, killing Malphas would be exceedingly difficult and costly. They would be reluctant to do so unless they were given no other choice.

When the others in Devil's Gate had demanded action, Malphas had taken Vetta into custody and held off her execution for a few days, not because of a sense of justice, but because of a sense of self preservation.

All of that told Duncan a few things. The first was that Malphas did not expect to suffer any repercussions from Thruvial's death because he hadn't been involved.

However, Malphas would be involved in Vetta's death if they hanged her.

He had to be sure that death wouldn't matter to anyone.

Duncan said, "This is the line you do not want to cross, Malphas."

The Djinn turned those supernova eyes back onto Duncan. "You have my attention, Vampyre. Explain what you mean."

"You may not belong to a particular House, but we do. Our House cares what happens to us, they know where we are and their associations are strong," Duncan said. "Carling Severan is my maker, and while she no longer sits on the Elder tribunal, she still maintains connections and alliances with the most Powerful of the Djinn. Those connections include the head of the tribunal itself, Soren, and Soren's son, Khalil of the House Marid. In fact you may have heard, once Carling and Khalil went to war together against a first generation pariah Djinn. They won."

"I see," said Malphas. His eyelids dropped over the blazing stars of his eyes, shuttering his expression.

Duncan told the Djinn, "Whatever happened to Thruvial is none of our concern. We are not here to solve a murder, to get involved or to placate the locals, no matter how much a sense of separateness or entitlement they seem to have acquired here at Devil's Gate. We don't have to justify taking an innocent girl away from a dangerous situation. You will not stop us from retrieving her, nor will you harm us in any way as we leave, because if you do, you would bring that kind of war down on yourself, and really, Malphas, when it comes right down to it, none of us are worth that to you."

As Duncan talked, a quick patter of footsteps sounded outside. The Vampyre guard appeared in the open doorway, carrying a backpack on one shoulder while she held onto the arm of a young medusa with a tear-streaked face.

The medusa screamed, "Aunt Serrie!"

"Let go of my niece," Seremela said. The Vampyre tossed the backpack to the floor and let go of Vetta who flung herself forward. Seremela snatched her close.

"You are quite right," said the pariah Djinn with an angelic smile. "None of you are worth that."

Seremela clenched the girl so hard the muscles in her arms jumped, while Vetta buried her face into her neck and sobbed. Seremela watched as the Djinn dissolved into black smoke that dissipated into nothing. Duncan pivoted on his heel toward her, his lean face composed but his eyes glittered with a dangerous light.

She said fiercely, "We're done here, right?"

"We're done," he said. He sounded as calm as he always did, his rich voice mellow and soothing, but as he strode toward her he pulled his gun.

She sucked air, held Vetta tighter and said between her teeth, "What now?"

Sympathy darkened Duncan's gaze as he reached her side. He gripped her shoulder and said, "Malphas has chosen to disengage, but that doesn't mean anybody else at Devil's Gate has."

"Shit," she muttered. Of course he was right. She looked around but the other Vampyre had disappeared as well.

Vetta lifted her head. Her eyes were smudged with streaks of black eyeliner, and her small, slender snakes were entirely subdued, curled quietly against her head. Seremela could see in her niece's young, exhausted face the ghost of the five-year-old Vetta had once been.

"I really need to go home now, Aunt Serrie," she whispered.

"Of course you do," she said gently. Now was not the time for recriminations or lectures. "Are you hurt?"

Vetta wiped at her face. "Just tired and hungry."

"All right." Seremela looked at the backpack that the Vampyre had tossed to the floor. "Is this yours?"

Vetta nodded. Duncan said, "We're not going to try to retrieve anything else. We're going straight to our car and leaving."

"That's fine, I don't care," said the girl, her voice wobbling. "I just want to get the hell out of here."

As Seremela turned her attention fully onto the backpack that Malphas's guard had tossed onto the floor, she immediately sensed a warm glow of aged Power. She bent and reached for the pack, scanning it carefully.

When she had been a medical examiner, most of the deaths she had autopsied had occurred through magical or Powerful means, and her magical sense was finely honed.

She was used to handling dangerous residual Power. Usually when she scanned for magic, she could compartmentalize it within moments. A spell cast by a human witch, an item infused with Dark Fae Power, Demonkind, Elven, Djinn or Light Fae—she knew the flavors and characteristics of all their magics, and most of the time she could either disable or contain the spells.

This, though. This was something different from anything she had ever encountered. The harder she concentrated, the deeper the well of Power felt underneath the veneer of that mild, mellow glow. For a moment she felt as though she might fall into something vaster than she had ever experienced.

Astonished and more than a little frightened, she jerked back and heard herself say sharply, "What do you have in there?"

"The goddamn Tarot deck from hell," Vetta said on a fresh sob.

She turned to stare at the girl. "Where on earth did you get something like that?"

Vetta's face twisted with a flash of her old rebellious self that crumpled quickly. She wailed, "I stole it a couple months ago.

I'm already so, so sorry I ever set eyes on it, so I don't need for you to yell at me about it right now, all right?"

Seremela angled her jaw out. She said in a soft, even tone of voice, "I can't help but notice your choice of words, Vetta. You're sorry you set eyes on it, but you're not sorry you stole it?"

The girl's reddened eyes widened with fresh dismay.

Duncan said quietly, "This conversation can wait until later. Seremela, is the pack too dangerous to take with us?"

She gave him a quick glance then turned her attention back to the pack. After a moment, she said, "It doesn't feel active at the moment, so I don't think so. It's a very old item of Power, though. We shouldn't just leave it."

"Then we'll take it," he said. "As long as you're willing to look after it and we leave right now."

She nodded, took the pack and slung it over one shoulder. Duncan strode to the trailer's open door and looked out. Moonlight edged his set expression and sharp gaze.

Seremela had grown accustomed reading to the subtle changes in his face. When she saw the line of his mouth harden, she asked, "What is it?"

"The only way out of this fenced-in enclosure is through the casino," he told her. "I noticed when we came in."

As soon as he mentioned it, she remembered the unbroken line of fence too.

She said to Vetta, "You keep your head down. You stick to me like glue, young lady, and above all, you keep quiet. I don't care if you see someone you don't like, or if someone says something you don't like. You do not antagonize anyone. Do you hear me?"

The girl bent her head and nodded, and Duncan led the way through the enclosure to the back of the casino, where bright flashes of color spilled out from the opening. It looked, Seremela thought uneasily, like the tent had been sliced open and was bleeding light.

They walked inside and along the main aisle.

Silence began to spread through the crowd. Seremela's stomach tightened as people stared at them. Then the whispering began. Vetta did as she had promised and kept her head down as she walked as close as she could get to Seremela without actually climbing on top of her.

Seremela put an arm around her niece's shoulders and several of her snakes wrapped around Vetta too. She tried as best as she could to adopt something of Duncan's calm, non-confrontational manner, while each step she took, each moment that passed, felt as though it took an hour. In vast contrast to how she had felt when they had come into the place, she glanced up at the armed Goblins on the walk overhead and felt grateful for their presence.

A ripple of reaction moved through the crowd like a wave, and she knew they weren't going to make it out of the casino without some kind of confrontation.

Duncan twisted to face the reaction. He still looked as prosaic as if he were taking out the trash, while her heart was jumping about in her chest like a cat on a hot tin roof. When she saw his lean, mildly interested profile, she felt a rush of emotion so powerful, it almost knocked her on her ass.

I love you, she thought. You have gone so far out of your way for me that you've traveled across the country. You've faced down petty criminals and a rogue Djinn. You accepted without question when I said that Vetta was innocent, and you've done all of it with humor and kindness, and you're willing to do even this for my niece, whom you haven't even been properly introduced to.

How could I not love you?

How could I not?

The crowd parted and a Dark Fae woman approached. She was tall and slim, with the trademark angular features and overlarge gray eyes of the Dark Fae. Her gleaming black hair was pulled back in a braid, and she wore simple dark leggings and a sleeveless tunic.

She also wore a sword that remained in its harness, strapped to her back. Her hands were empty and lax at her sides as she came face to face with them.

Vetta broke her promise of silence in a whisper. "Xanthe."

Seremela's arm tightened on her in warning.

Other than a slight smile and crinkling of her eyes, an expression that was gone almost before Seremela had registered it, the Dark Fae woman gave no sign that she heard Vetta. Instead she turned to Duncan and said, "Please allow me to assist in escorting you safely from this place."

"Why should we?" Duncan asked.

"Because I, too, know that the girl is innocent," said the Dark Fae. She spoke English perfectly, with a trace of accent, and raised her voice as she said it, causing another reaction to ripple through the avid-looking onlookers.

"Then by all means," said Duncan, as he gestured to the aisle in front of him.

"After you."

The woman Vetta had called Xanthe inclined her head and took the lead, while Duncan fell back. He gestured for Seremela and Vetta to go ahead of him, and he came up close behind them.

Warily, Seremela followed the Dark Fae woman, while she tried to think how the maneuver might possibly be a trap, but she couldn't see how—the woman had, after all, made very public declaration of Vetta's innocence and support.

They worked their way through the rest of the casino. With the Dark Fae ahead of them, and Duncan guarding them from behind, Seremela felt marginally more secure. She devoutly hoped it wasn't an illusion.

She asked Vetta telepathically, "*Do you know this woman?*"

"*Not really,*" the girl said. "*I know who she is—or was, anyway. She was one of Thruvial's attendants. He had three. I guess that's traditional?*"

Vetta was correct. Dark Fae triads were quite traditional and appeared in various forms in their society. Seremela wondered where Thruvial's other two attendants were.

She said, "*Yes, it is. What do you know about her?*"

Vetta shrugged. She looked and sounded exhausted. "*Like I said, nothing much. She's quiet and keeps to herself.*"

"*Okay,*" Seremela said.

They fell silent. Later Seremela would have dreams about that hellish walk through Gehenna, the dreams filled with a creeping sense of dread while a host of creatures stared at her with hungry gazes and stalked close behind her, moving in for a kill.

Then finally they stepped out of the tent. The cooler desert night air outside was indescribably wonderful. Seremela and Vetta took deep breaths, almost staggering with relief, as the Dark Fae woman paused to look over her shoulder at them.

"Don't stop," murmured Duncan. "We need to go quickly."

Seremela nodded, and their small group moved into a different formation. This time the Dark Fae woman fell back to walk at Seremela's side, while Duncan moved up beside Vetta on the other side.

The Dark Fae woman said, "We should not go through the crowded part toward the center of the camp. It is quieter along the outskirts."

Duncan and Seremela looked at Vetta for confirmation. The girl said, "Xanthe's right. The camp's quieter around the edges."

"Show us," Duncan said.

Both Vetta and the Dark Fae woman did, and they were able to move quickly through the quiet, shadowed area. They had circumvented the encampment and reached the edge of the massive parking lot when Seremela couldn't keep quiet any longer.

She stopped, pulling Vetta to a halt. The other two stopped as well.

Seremela said to the Dark Fae woman, "You. What is your name?"

"Xanthe Tenanye," replied the Dark Fae.

"You just left her there," Seremela said. "You knew Vetta was innocent, and you let them imprison her for—what, two days? She was terrified and all alone."

"I did not leave her," said Xanthe. Her large gray eyes seemed to gather all the meager illumination from the moonlight, while her hands remained at her sides. "I stayed in Gehenna for the last two days, watching while I tried to figure out what I could do for her. I would not have let them hang her."

"Interesting," said Duncan. He had moved so that he was much closer to the Dark Fae. "How did you know Vetta was innocent, and how would you have stopped it?"

"By confessing, if I had no other choice," said Xanthe Tenanye. "I knew Vetta didn't kill Cieran Thruvial, because I did."

"You're a killer?" Vetta said it with such a squeak of surprise it would have sounded comical in almost any other situation.

"You may call me such, if you must," said Xanthe.

"What are you still doing here?" Vetta asked. "They will hang you, if they realize you did it."

"I am well aware of that, but I was not free to leave until you were," said Xanthe. She looked around. "It is not safe to stay here and have this conversation. You still need to leave immediately."

Seremela and Duncan looked at each other. He murmured, "Understanding what happened or getting involved is still not our mission."

"My thoughts exactly," Seremela said grimly. She remembered where they had parked the SUV and started hauling Vetta in that direction.

That was when Vetta chose to dig in her heels, literally. By simply not moving, she dragged Seremela to a stop. "Why?" Vetta said raggedly to Xanthe. "They held me in a metal building without food or water, and I knew I was going to die. All of that was because you murdered someone, and I need to know why."

For the first time since she had approached them, Xanthe exposed emotion in her body language as she shifted sharply and rubbed the back of her neck. Then she said abruptly, "I work for the Dark Fae Queen. More accurately, I work for her chief of security. I didn't just murder Thruvial, I executed him on orders for crimes committed against the crown. I had no idea that you would get blamed for his death. Now will you go?"

As soon as the Dark Fae woman mentioned the Queen, Seremela and Duncan jerked to a halt. They stared at Xanthe.

"Oh hell," said Duncan. "She's telling the truth."

Seremela was beginning to feel dizzy from all the shifts in reality over the last few hours.

Murder. Illegal drugs. A pariah, and now inter-demesne politics. Oh, and she couldn't forget to add theft of a major item of Power to that list, not when its subtle, fathomless Power was slowly but surely soaking into the bones of her shoulder. It felt good, nourishing and exotic at the same time, and she didn't trust that feeling one iota.

Vetta had started to speak. Seremela interrupted her. "No more discussion." She had never used such a harsh tone of voice with her niece before. Vetta looked shocked and her mouth shut with a snap. Seremela steered her niece back around in the direction of their SUV as she said to Xanthe, "Thank you for watching out for my niece. Either come with us now or stay, and goodbye."

Duncan moved to Seremela's side with smooth, liquid grace. Xanthe took a few steps backward as she said, "My thanks, but you would be much safer withou—"

A new voice interrupted her. "We could not believe it, Xanthe, when we heard that you defended our lord's murderer and escorted her from Gehenna. Now we see your betrayal with our very own eyes."

For the second time that night, Duncan blurred. By the time Seremela had spun around, he already faced the two newcomers with his gun aimed at their heads.

They were Dark Fae, a male and a female, dressed like Xanthe in simple leggings and sleeveless tunics, with swords strapped to their backs. They stared from Xanthe to Vetta and Seremela, their expressions bitter with hate.

"She is innocent," said Xanthe as she drew her sword. "They will pass from this place unharmed."

"She's poison," spat the male. "She made no secret of how she loathed our lord, and now she has brought another of her kind who is even more poisonous." He and his companion drew their swords as well, and the sound of the long scrape of metal ran down Seremela's spine.

"Do they not comprehend that you have a gun trained on them?" Seremela said incredulously in Duncan's head.

Xanthe lunged, the others stepped to meet her and the clash of steel rang out.

"I can't use it and they know it," said Duncan. *"The gun-shot would draw too much attention. The sound of the swordfight is bad enough."*

He tossed the gun at her. Shocked, she made an incoherent noise and let go of Vetta to stumble forward, just barely managing to catch it.

"I hope you can shoot," Duncan told her. "Use it as a last resort."

She stared at him, caught the moonlit edge of his shadowed smile, and then he sprang at the three fighting Dark Fae.

Vetta was whispering, "Oh gods, I just want to wake up and be in my own bed."

Seremela's hands shook as she checked the 9 mm. Duncan had put it on safety before he tossed it to her. She clicked it off and stood ready as she watched the fight. While she was by no means an expert, yes, she knew how to shoot.

"Get behind me," she told Vetta. The girl obeyed and huddled shivering against her back. All of Seremela's snakes focused on the danger in front of her. Every muscle in her body was pulled as taut as piano wire, and she felt slightly nauseous as she tried to make sense of the melee.

They were so fast, all four of them, faster than she could track, and the Dark Fae were so difficult to tell apart in the silvery shadows. One struck another—oh, it was a bad blow—and that one grunted and went down on both knees, while Duncan engaged the third in a vicious flurry of blows and countermoves, and the fight

was horribly, sickeningly unfair because his opponent
had a sword while all he had was his knife.

A tic started at her temple, fluttering at a frenetic
pace, because it was one thing to know how to shoot but
quite another to know who to shoot, and just how was
she supposed to tell when the last resort was, anyway?

She pushed the heel of one hand against her temple
as she tracked Duncan's opponent with the gun.

Duncan leaped forward, a fast, vicious attack. His
opponent fell back and kept falling until he lay prone on
the ground. It took a couple of heartbeats for Seremela
to comprehend what had happened, because the violence
ended as quickly and abruptly as it had started.

Two of the Dark Fae were down. Duncan and the
third faced each other but didn't leap to attack each
other. Seremela only recognized Xanthe for certain as
the other woman reached over her head to sheathe her
sword.

She lowered the gun, slid the safety back on and
strode rapidly over to Duncan to fling her arms around
him. He clenched her to him, one hand at the back of
her neck.

"You're not hurt?" she whispered.

"No," he whispered back. "I'm all right."

Oh gods, thank you. She held onto him with all of her
strength.

His lean cheek was cool against hers, the length of
his body hard. He said, "Let's go home now."

She nodded. She couldn't trust herself to speak. In that moment, she thought those were the four most wonderful words in the English language.

Let's go home now.

Chapter Seven

Hearth

After a nerve wracking yet uneventful drive back to the Reno airport, they were airborne a couple of hours later and headed to Chicago where they would stop just long enough to allow Xanthe to disembark before they flew to Miami.

During the car trip Vetta drank three bottles of water, ate a couple of protein bars and had a crying jag against Seremela's shoulder as relief set in. As soon as they had cell phone reception, they called Seremela's sister, Camilla, and Vetta cried some more at her mother. Once they boarded the jet and took off, the girl disappeared into the lavatory for a while to emerge some time later, looking pale and exhausted but somewhat cleaner.

After Vetta finished, they all took turns washing up. Seremela sighed with relief as she rinsed the desert dust off her face, arms and neck.

Dawn spilled over the horizon. After shuttering all of the windows to block out the morning sun, the co-pilot served Xanthe, Vetta and Seremela bistro-style breakfast trays with fresh fruit, rolls, cheese, hard boiled eggs and smoked salmon, hot coffee and cream and fresh squeezed orange juice.

Duncan accepted a glass of bloodwine. Seremela frowned. After a sleepless, stressful night she was starving. He must be too. While bloodwine might do in a pinch, it did not have nearly the same nutritive qualities as fresh blood did.

Somewhat haltingly, she asked him, *"Will bloodwine be—sufficient for you, for now? I would be honored to help if you need fresh blood."*

Duncan smiled at her. He looked inexplicably sweet and roguish, and she thought he even looked somewhat embarrassed. Although she wasn't sure what prompted his expression, she could not help but smile back.

"That is very kind of you," he said. *"Bloodwine will be sufficient for now, thank you."*

She felt her cheeks warm and her gaze slid away from his. She had never fed a Vampyre directly from her vein before. Their bites were famous for inducing a sense of euphoria in their donors. Perhaps that was why he looked embarrassed. She glanced at Xanthe and Vetta. It was probably just as well he didn't need fresh blood at the moment.

Even though tiredness threatened to take her over, she ate quickly and drank several cups of coffee, fueled by a sense of purpose. She was not going to relax while they carried an unexamined item of Power on the plane.

As she ate, she listened to Duncan and Xanthe talk. Duncan asked, "Why kill Thruvial instead of taking him back to face trial?"

"He was the last nobleman involved in the conspiracy that killed the Queen's family," Xanthe said. "The problem with putting him on trial was that the evidence we managed to gather might not have been enough to convict him. Lord Black Eagle made the decision on the kill order."

The unfamiliar name caused Seremela to pause, until she realized that Xanthe referred to Tiago, the Wyr warlord who had mated with Niniane. She had met Tiago when she had been a medical examiner in Chicago, and she shuddered as she recalled Tiago's edgy demeanor. He had terrified her—she had no problem whatsoever imagining him taking responsibility for ordering someone's execution.

The Dark Fae woman was continuing. "It took me the better part of the year to work my way into Thruvial's household. He fled Adriyel as soon as the borders opened. The trials of his fellow conspirators had shaken him considerably, but it didn't stop him from committing other distasteful crimes at Devil's Gate—including sex trafficking, protection and blackmail."

"He was a horrible man," Vetta whispered, her head bent.

Seremela murmured gently, "Did he hurt you in any way?"

Vetta looked at her sidelong, and she could tell her niece knew what she was really asking. Vetta shook her head and told her telepathically, "*He thought I was disgusting, but he wanted to put me out to customers who were interested in exotic experiences. The last time we talked—fought, actually—he threatened to scar my face if I didn't do as he said. I'm glad he's dead."*

Seremela breathed evenly, struggling to contain her rage as she listened. *"I'm glad he's dead too,"* she said.

She finished her breakfast, swallowed her last cup of coffee, set the breakfast tray aside and reached for Vetta's backpack. "Don't relax too much yet," she said to her niece who was drooping sideways in her seat. "You need to tell me about this Tarot deck from hell. Who did you steal it from?"

"I don't know," Vetta said. "She was just some woman at a rest stop. I lifted it from the back of her car when she went inside the gas station. I could tell it had a tingle of Power. At first I thought it was cool. Then every time I started to lay out a spread for myself, Death kept showing up. Every time, Aunt Serrie. It got so that I couldn't sleep. I kept checking the cards. Then I started to pray. I was so sure I was going to die." Her voice broke at the end.

Seremela touched the back of Vetta's hand in silent sympathy. Vetta watched miserably as Seremela searched through the pack, and Duncan and Xanthe grew quiet to watch too.

The pack didn't hold anything of much value. A couple packs of Marlboro Reds, a cigarette lighter, a scarf that smelled like patchouli and smoke, some cosmetics, a wallet with Vetta's I.D. and some cash. It was unusual that nobody had taken the cash or the Tarot cards themselves, but she suspected that employees who worked for Malphas were scrupulously careful about their conduct.

A wooden box lay at the bottom of the pack. She pulled it out and set it on the table. It was clearly the source of the glow of Power. The box's lid had a hand-painted, stylized face. One side of the face was male, the other side female. It was Taliesin, the god of the Dance.

She opened the box, pulled out the deck of cards and turned over the top one, a Major Arcana card. A picture of a golden woman, in a chariot with seven lions, smiled up at her. Inanna, the goddess of Love. She turned over a few of other cards, and each one was exquisite.

Aside from being an item of Power, the deck was a work of art. *Oh, Vetta.*

She sighed and rubbed her forehead while she studied the deck.

Her initial impression remained the same. Underneath the veneer of quiet Power, the cards held a subtle but remarkable depth. Finally she sat back and shook her head, her mouth tight.

"I have no idea whose magic created this," she said. "It's not Light or Dark Fae, Elven, Wyr, Demonkind, human—or anything else I've encountered. It's more Powerful than it looks on the surface, and I'm not even sure what the Power does. Perhaps it's just meant to be a tool for divination. I don't know." She met Duncan's gaze as she said, "I don't sense anything overtly offensive in the magic, but I don't like magic I don't understand, and I don't trust it."

Xanthe reached out to touch one of the cards, her gray eyes wide. She said, "I think they're beautiful."

As the tips of Xanthe's long fingers touched the card, Seremela felt the Power in the deck pull toward the other woman. She said sharply, "Do you feel that?"

All three of the others stared at her and shook their heads. Vetta sat as far back from the deck as she could get, her hands tucked under her arms. Duncan asked, "What did you feel?"

"It's tugging toward you, like it wants to go to you," Seremela said to Xanthe.

"Oh please take the deck with you," said Vetta passionately. "Please take it far, far away."

Seremela didn't want to take responsibility for the Tarot deck, and Vetta refused to touch it. Xanthe was willing to take the Tarot deck to Adriyel, to see if she could discover any answers about its origins and its maker from Dark Fae elders, so in the end that was what they decided to do.

The Dark Fae woman disembarked at Chicago's O'Hare with quiet thanks.

As soon as the plane was in the air again, Vetta sprawled on the couch and fell asleep as soon as she went horizontal.

Duncan and Seremela moved to the back of the plane so that they didn't disturb the sleeping girl. He settled in the seat beside Seremela. She looked exhausted, with dark shadows under her eyes, but her gaze was clear and bright. She whispered, "I cannot thank you enough, Duncan."

"Shh," he said, just as softly. "There's no need."

"There's every need," she said, her words quiet but forceful. Her mouth worked, and her expression was so beautiful, so intense, Duncan had to put his arms around her and kiss her.

Her mouth. It was like everything else about her, sensitive and lavish with softness yet etched with determination and character.

He loved her mouth; he loved it and he kissed and kissed her, while she twined her arms around his neck and kissed him back. Roused by her gentle, heartfelt response, his sexual aggression was lying in wait, ready to pounce. He held it tightly in check. Now was not the time.

Reluctantly he pulled away, and laughter threatened to take him over as he realized all of her snakes had wrapped around him again. He smiled into her gorgeous eyes. "Why do you always look so surprised whenever I touch you?"

She glanced away as she lifted a shoulder. "Many people are disgusted by the thought of touching us, much like Thruvial was with Vetta."

"Thruvial was a pig," Duncan said. That jerked her attention back to him. He said deliberately into her wide gaze, "I think you are the most beautiful woman I've ever met, inside and out."

Wonder lightened her feminine features. "You do?"

"I do. I learned a lot about you in a day."

"It was a long day," she pointed out.

He laughed softly. "It was a very long day. You're intelligent and curious, insightful and adventurous, and you're generous and caring. Even though you're gentle to the bone, you know how to shoot a gun, and you're so brave, especially when you're frightened." His smile turned crooked. "I hope you don't mind that I'm falling in love with you."

There it was again, that look of hers, stricken with wonder and trembling at the threshold of delight. She breathed, "I don't mind in the slightest."

"That's all right then." Because he had tensed up as he waited for her response, he relaxed and pressed a kiss to her forehead. "Did you know that *Rigoletto* is playing this season?"

She nestled close with a sigh. "I love Verdi's operas."

"I'll get us tickets," he promised, resting his cheek against her temple.

They grew quiet, and after a while Duncan thought she fell asleep. He couldn't. He was too full of the fabulous sensation of her curvaceous, warm body pressed against his side. He closed his eyes and drifted quietly, letting his imagination have free rein.

He wanted to do things with her. He wanted to talk over morning newspapers, hold hands in a movie theater, walk along the beach on a full moonlit night. He wanted her to call him and interrupt him while he was at work. He wanted to watch her enjoy a good meal.

He wanted to suckle her to climax, and spear into her soft body until he climaxed. He wanted to fall asleep in her arms.

He wanted to bite her so fucking bad.

He was so absorbed in the dark red of sensual anticipation, she shocked him utterly when she whispered against his neck, "I love you too."

Gods.

He'd known emptiness in his life, and he knew how to be alone. He'd had taken lovers for a time and then they had parted, and he had watched his human friends and family die. He had never known anyone to fill him up so completely by saying four of the most beautiful words in any language.

I love you too.

No longer immersed in a dark red quiet, he discovered himself in a place of shining light.

Seremela's sister, Camilla, flew in from Atlanta. She was waiting for them at the airport in Miami when they arrived that afternoon. Camilla and Vetta fell sobbing into each other's arms, and after a moment Camilla turned to Seremela and roped her into the embrace. Hands in his pockets, Duncan stood back to give the women a little space. He grinned at the look Seremela gave him as she succumbed to Camilla's clutching hug.

Then it was his turn. "Thank you," Camilla said as she gripped both his hands. "Thank you so much. I—I feel like there's more I should say, but I just don't have the words."

"We'll meet properly some other time," Duncan told Seremela's sister. "In the meantime, you are most welcome. Enjoy having your daughter back safe and sound."

Seremela told her sister, "Vetta will fill you in on everything. I'm too tired to talk."

Camilla said, "I'll call you tomorrow?"

"That's fine." Seremela staggered as Vetta threw her arms around her, hugging her fiercely. They stood for a moment in intense silence. Whatever they said to each other was telepathic, meant for each other alone, which Duncan thought was fitting.

After Camilla and Vetta left, a valet brought his car around while Seremela turned awkward and tried to explain how she could take a taxi home. Duncan listened patiently then said, "Don't be silly. Of course I will see you home."

She gave him a deer-in-the-headlights look. He was so amused and intrigued by it, he strode two steps forward until his chest brushed the tips of her delicious breasts and he growled into her upturned face, "We have unfinished business."

Her tremulous mouth formed two silent words. "We do?"

Falling in love was a beautiful feeling, as long as he fell with her. He grinned and bent his head until their lips touched. Then he said silently into her parted lips, *"We do."*

The drive to her home was completed in fiery silence. She couldn't sit still and fidgeted, and her snakes roamed restlessly around her.

He didn't want her to sit still. He wanted her to fidget and flutter about, while he stalked his prey to capture her finally, finally—against a door, cabinet, couch, wherever the hell, it didn't matter, any of the images his heated imagination supplied him were just fine, because he would capture her, it was just a matter of time. The red darkness took him over, and he held himself under savage control as he drove with immaculate care through the heavy Friday Miami traffic.

Fear and violence always touched a Vampyre's life somehow. He had never realized how he had grown used to it, until he faced that goddamn pariah Djinn and grew shocked at Seremela facing danger and violence. She was too good, too fine; she loved opera and classic movies, and she lived in a civilized, lawful world, and she should never, ever have to face such violence again.

Dimly he realized he was allowing himself to react to what had happened, and by letting go, he was no longer in control.

The atmosphere in the car had grown excruciatingly charged by the time he drove into the underground garage at her apartment building. He pulled into a parking space. The quiet purr of the car engine faded. Seremela started to say something, her words stumbling and awkward.

Staring straight ahead, he interrupted her. "Invite me in."

She took in a quick breath. It shook a little, and his cock hardened at the small telltale sign. He turned to her and discovered her staring at him with that wide eyed, wondering look. Three of her snakes peered sideways from behind her head, staring at him too.

Laughter spilled out of him as the sight broke his tension. He reached out to one of the snakes. It touched the tip of his finger with a light flicker of its tongue. He repeated unsteadily, "Invite me in, Seremela. Please."

"I would love for you to come in," she whispered all in a rush.

With that, he lost all capacity for words or coherent thought. Somehow they got out of the car and into the elevator, where he backed her into a corner. He planted one hand on the wall on either side of her head and stared into her eyes as he breathed in the scent of her arousal. Her breathing grew choppy, and he watched the muscles in her slender throat move as she swallowed, the iridescent pattern that marked her skin shimmering in the overhead light.

Her lovely, slender throat.

His fangs descended. His face twisted as he fought himself. This was too far out of control. He was a stranger to himself.

Her warm, trembling hands smoothed the material of his T-shirt across his chest. "It's all right," she whispered. "I want you to bite me."

He hadn't even been aware that he'd taken a useless breath of air until it rushed out of him. The force of his own reaction nearly sent him to his knees.

"Duncan," she said. She sounded and looked dazed.

He lowered his head slowly, and ran his mouth along the leaping pulse at her neck, tonguing the delectable delicate flesh.

She pushed him, startling him out of his preoccupation. With a husky, drunken laugh, she pointed behind him. He looked over his shoulder. The elevator doors stood open. Ah, right.

The length of the hallway to her front door was all but unendurable. He said hoarsely, "After we go to the opera, what are we doing next?"

"I don't know," she moaned. She dropped her keys and bent over to retrieve them. "How about a weekend in bed?"

He blurred, snatched the keys out from underneath her hand and unlocked and opened her door before she could fully react. "Get inside."

He glared as she exploded with laughter. Then he laughed too. This was crazy, ludicrous. He could say he hadn't felt this way since he was a teenager, except he was certain he hadn't felt this way then either.

Then finally they were inside, alone in her shadowed apartment. She tossed her purse onto the couch—he realized they had forgotten her case, in the trunk of his car—and then he lost that thought too as she leaped at him. He snatched her up as she wrapped her arms and legs around him, and he strode for the bedroom.

"Say it again," he said. "What you told me on the plane."

Her brilliantly colorful eyes were luminous with emotion and desire. "I didn't think you heard me."

He laid her on the bed gently and straightened. He tore off his shirt. "I heard you. Say it again."

She pushed up to kneel on the bed in front of him, and she met his gaze as she reached for the fastening of his jeans. "I love you, Duncan."

"That was even better than the last time," he whispered, smiling as he palmed her full, soft breast. She pulled his jeans open and slid her hands inside them as she eased the material down over his lean hips. An odd sensation slid along his torso and up his arms. He glanced down at her snakes as they journeyed across his skin.

Seremela followed the direction of his gaze and drew back a little, her expression turning self-conscious. She offered softly, "I can wrap them, if you'd rather."

He said firmly, "No."

She pulled a few snakes away from him. "Are you sure it isn't too—tentacley for you?"

He grasped her shoulders and looked deeply into her eyes. "Listen to me. I did not say I was falling in love with you, if only you would hide some part of yourself or change some aspect to try to please me. I said I was falling in love with you—all of you. I don't want you to curb yourself, deny yourself, cover up your face or head or any part of your body. I don't want you to lose or gain weight, or watch what you say, or deny how you feel, or try to be anything but who you are, because who you are is the most beautiful person in the world to me."

As she listened, the expression on her lovely features grew vulnerable, wide open. While he certainly hoped that he had not been the first person to ever tell her such things, he selfishly hoped that he had been the first male to do so. He grasped one of her snakes, kissed it on the nose and looked into its face. "You're never going to bite me, are you?"

"They would never hurt you," Seremela said. "They would die first."

"Oh well," he said, giving her a crooked grin. "There's goes that fantasy."

Her eyes went very wide, and she laughed, a joyous, surprised sound. She unbuttoned her top and shrugged out of it then slipped off her bra as Duncan kicked off his jeans and stood nude, his heavy erection jutting from his hips.

Her breasts were stunning, lush and full, the soft, plump nipples several shades darker than the light creamy green of her flesh. He bent, took one nipple in his mouth and sucked at it gently. The muffled noise that came out of her was urgent and incoherent. She cradled his head, ran her fingers through his hair and stroked his shoulders.

As he suckled her, a feather light sensation flickered along the sensitive skin on the head of his penis, creating a sharp, tantalizing pleasure. He looked down, as the sensation spread along the tight, drawn up sac of his testicles, and along the muscles of his lower abdomen.

Seremela's snakes flickered their slender tongues along his skin.

Seremela cocked her head and looked down as well. "They're tasting you," she said, giving him a sidelong smile. "They know that I love you, and they're curious." She looked splendid and barbaric, and completely unfettered.

For a moment, the ghost of the human Duncan once was struggled with the image. But Seremela's snakes were not mundane creatures; they were a part of her, and Duncan had not been human for a very long time.

His fangs descended. Seremela looked at his mouth and her gaze turned heavy lidded. She bared her neck to him in wordless invitation, and he gathered her soft, curvaceous body into his arms and eased his fangs gently into the pulse at her neck.

The moan that came out of her was full of sex and surrender, the sound shivering along his heated senses as hot blood spilled into his mouth, and it was so strange, so strange. He was twisted up inside, his desire for her out of control. He growled as he drank from her, while she arched against him, gasping. Her blood was stronger than human blood. It punched through him and made the world spin.

He lifted his head away from her, breathing raggedly, and only then realized she was struggling in his arms. For a terrible moment he felt sickened and disoriented—until he realized what she was trying to do.

"Help me get out of these damn jeans," she whimpered.

His fingers shook as he helped her to ease the jeans down to her knees. Then she lay back on bed and raised her legs so he could tug them off the rest of the way.

Wholly naked, she stretched, her eyes glazed with the lingering pleasure from his bite, and she looked beautiful and mysterious at once, all woman and wholly inhuman. He stroked his fingers up her inner thigh and fingered the velvet soft petals of her sex that were already wet with pleasure. She grasped his cock in one hand, stroking it as she parted her legs and told him, "Come inside now."

"I want to help you climax first," he whispered. He found her stiff little bud, so delicate and luscious, and he rolled the ball of his thumb over it.

She jerked uncontrollably and gasped. "It feels too good. It's too intense."

"That's partly from the bite," he crooned. "Everything's more intense right now." He slid two fingers into her, and she was softer and wetter than anything he had ever felt before, and so goddamn snug, he knew when he finally entered her, she was going to grip him tighter than a fist. He fucked her gently with his fingers while he continued to massage her clitoris.

"I can't take it," she sobbed. She gripped his wrist.

"You can take it," he told her. While he worked her, he bent over to take her nipple in his mouth again, suckling at her carefully because his fangs were still descended and he did not want to scratch her. He was drowning in his own pleasure, drowning, immersed in her escalating pleasure as she undulated her hips.

Then she put a hand to the back of his head and pulled him down hard against her breast. His fangs broke the tender skin at her breast, and her Powerful blood filled his mouth again. Astonished, he sucked her hard while he drove his fingers into her, and she bucked underneath his hold and screamed as she climaxed.

He was blind with his own euphoria and still throbbing with need. He held himself rigidly, his palm pressed firmly against her clit while her inner muscles pulsed against his fingers. He would not draw out, not leave her until her climax was done, but then she shocked him again as she pulled his hand away. She rose and pushed him onto his back, and as he acquiesced, she came up over him and straddled him. She was the most amazing sight he had ever seen, her beautiful face stamped with intensity as she took his cock, positioned him and lowered herself down on him.

"Jesus," he said. His own climax shot like a bullet. He gripped her hips and bucked hard underneath her, swearing.

She collapsed on him, and he hugged her with his whole body. After a few minutes, she asked, "We're going to do this a lot, aren't we?"

"God, I hope so," he said.

They slept just like that, with him still inside of her and her sprawled like a rag doll on him.

He woke first. His erection had softened, and he didn't want to move and slip outside of her or wake her up. She was a soft, warm weight lying on him, and he loved it, loved it.

So he drifted a while and let his mind meander. Maybe she liked jewelry.

Maybe she would enjoy a ring.

Maybe she would enjoy it especially if he went down on one knee to give it to her.

He had always thought he would enjoy marriage, and he believed he would make a good husband for the right woman. He had just never found the right woman, until now.

But he was getting way ahead of himself. They hadn't even gone on their first date yet. Speaking of which, he had opera tickets to buy.

Wait. He yawned and asked, "What day is it?"

"Nnh." Just when he was sure she had fallen back asleep, she murmured, "Think it's Friday?"

"Excellent. I think our first date should start right now."

She scratched her nose. "You don't have opera tickets yet."

"That's going to have to be our second date," he told her.

She opened her eyes and squinted at him. "What's our first date?"

He rolled her onto her back, reversing their positions, and grinned down at her. "My vote is for that weekend in bed."

She snickered. "Ooh, that's my vote too. At some point we should call Carling and Rune and tell them we're back."

"We can do that Monday." He palmed her breast as his cock stiffened against her thigh. "We should also plan our third date soon."

"Mm, we should." Her gaze grew heavy lidded as she fingered his penis.

"I'm so glad to be back in my own bed."

"I'm glad to be in your bed too." He moved his hips lazily, pushing against her hand.

Her expression softened with equal parts pleasure and affection. "So do you have any ideas about that third date?"

Duncan cocked his head, considering her. He thought about telling her about buying a ring, and him going down on one knee, but he didn't want to spook her. Instead he said, very casually, "I thought we might go shopping."

"You like to shop?" she asked in sleepy surprise.

"Yes, I do, sometimes. When I know I'm looking for something special." He bent to nuzzle her throat.

She made a purring sound and stroked his back. "It sounds like you've got something specific in mind for your shopping trip."

"Our shopping trip," he corrected.

"Okay, our shopping trip."

"And I do have something specific in mind, but for now, I think we should focus on our first date."

Giddy with happiness, he kissed her in a soft lingering caress. They lived in a crowded and dangerous world, but somehow she had become the only person in it.

Right here and now, they were the only two people in the world, the only two.

"Duncan, do you by any chance play the piano?" she murmured.

He chuckled. "Why on earth would you ask me that?" She stroked his face. "You just gave me a certain look." Amused, he asked, "A look that said I play the piano?"

She tapped his nose with one finger. "Tell me you have a Bogart suit. Oh forget it, you have lots of suits, and they're all more beautiful than any of the clothes I own. Do you by any chance believe in precognition?"

He announced, "I am completely at sea in this conversation."

"Then we should probably stop talking," she whispered. She rolled her hips at him.

"I'm okay with that," he said.

He proceeded to make love to her again on their most excellent first date, and neither one said anything coherent for a long time.

Hunter's Season

Author's Note

Dear Readers,

I loved writing Hunter's Season for several reasons. In it I was able to wrap up the story arc of the mysterious Elder Races Tarot deck, and I was also able to, at long last, return to the Dark Fae land of Adriyel to catch up a little with Tiago and Niniane, the hero and heroine from *Storm's Heart*. This story also gave me the chance to give two very deserving people, Aubrey and Xanthe, a HEA (happily ever after) ending after their long, hard journeys.

You will also find a small HEA for a cameo character, a six year old Wyr housecat nicknamed Mouse, who has had her own rough journey. This character was the creation of the winner of my "Create an Elder Races Character" contest, in which many of you entered wonderfully creative inventions. I had huge fun taking the details of this small character and weaving them into the story, and I hope you have just as much fun reading about her.

Because of your enthusiasm and continued interest, I would love to dedicate this story to you, the readers.

Thank you so very much.

Wishing you many hours of happy reading,
Thea

Chapter One

Hearth

As soon as Xanthe reached Adriyel, she left her mount at the palace stable and sent a message to Her Majesty's Chief of Security that said: "It is done."

Xanthe did not sign the note. He would know who had sent it. She did not expect a quick response either. With the completion of her assignment, any urgency or need for action had ceased.

Because she had been gone to America for some time, she stopped at the marketplace to buy food: fresh bread, meat, eggs, vegetables and fruit. The familiarity of the task soothed nerves that were tired and stressed from living with too much strangeness and danger for so long.

At midafternoon, the best of the goods had already been picked over, but there was still enough variety to meet her immediate needs. The market stalls were stocked with meat and fish, vegetables, fruit and grains from nearby farms, a variety of cooked foods, beautiful cloths of rich colors and intricate needlework, pottery, spices, soaps and metal work, and the recent, jarring addition of American goods. Hawkers called their wares, and the smells of cooking food wafted along the narrow cobblestone streets.

Xanthe paused as the small creature she carried in her pack stirred. A small creature might be too hungry to wait until she had cooked supper. After a moment's thought, she backtracked to the baker's stall to buy a meat pie. Her last purchase was an earthenware jug of fresh milk and a small tub of soft cheese. When she had finished the milk and the cheese, she would return the jug and the tub to the dairyman.

The wriggling in her pack became more urgent.

"Patience," she said to it.

Then she walked out of the city, down the narrow road that hugged the river for a couple of miles to the overgrown path that led to the small two-room cottage that had been her home for her entire life. Ignoring the increasingly strong wriggles in the pack on her back, she studied the cottage as she approached. It had a neglected air about it, as well it should, since she had been gone for over four seasons, but the roof looked solid enough. It led her to hope that the inside was dry.

She opened the door and looked into the shadowed, dusty interior. For a moment, it all looked too rustic, small and strange. Then the strangeness of the last several moons—months, they were called in America—fell from her eyes, and the cottage became once again as familiar to her as the back of her own hand, and she was home.

She remembered something a human had once said to her while she had been in the strange tent city at

Devil's Gate in the American state named Nevada. The human had been sunburned and had worn a cynical expression when he said, "You know how that old saying goes—you can't go home again."

Xanthe had never been to America before, and she didn't know how the saying went. She wasn't sure what the human had meant.

She eased her packages onto the dusty table, shrugged out of her pack and set it carefully on the floor, and took off the shoulder harness that carried her sword, straightening tired shoulders. The day had already been full of travel, and there was still much to do before she could rest that night.

She propped the door open to the fresh, cooling air of the evening. Now the small creature in her pack was voicing shrill unhappiness. It sounded like a crying baby. She opened the pack and pulled out a thin, wriggling orange striped kitten that leaped out of her hands onto the table and circled the wrapped meat pie and dairy, meowing piteously.

"Yes, I know," Xanthe told it. "But you must wait a moment or two longer."

She had fallen into the habit of talking to the kitten on the trip from the crossover passage to Adriyel. They had developed a habit of sorts in the evenings on the short three day journey—the kitten would fall asleep, purring, either on her lap or beside the campfire while Xanthe studied the lovely hand painted cards of the Tarot deck she had been given by a Vampyre and two medusae on her trip to Chicago, to the crossover passageway that led back home.

People in America had such an odd term for places like Adriyel. They called them Other lands, but to Xanthe, America was the Other land.

Most of the time the kitten seemed to enjoy the sound of her voice, but it wasn't interested in conversation at the moment. It swatted at the pie and meowed again, showing slender sharp white teeth and a tiny pink tongue.

Xanthe checked the cupboard that held the crockery. Along with all the other furniture in the cottage, her father had built the cupboard well out of hard seasoned wood. No small creatures had taken up residence in it, so she wiped out a bowl with the bottom of her sleeve, poured some milk into it and set it on the floor.

As the purring kitten leaped down and began to lap at the creamy liquid, she unwrapped and broke open the meat pie. It was still hot. Fragrant steam rose from the middle. She scraped meat and gravy onto a dish, blew on it until it had cooled slightly and set it on the floor by the bowl of milk.

While the kitten gorged itself on supper, Xanthe set to work. She dusted and swept out spiders and a few mice nests. With the kitten as a mouser, they wouldn't be back. Then she brought in half rotted wood from the small pile left under the lean-to, started a fire, uncovered the well and drew water, diced the raw meat and vegetables into a pot and set it over the fire to cook, washed the table and chairs, dragged the mattress out of the simple bedroom and beat it until the clouds of dust stopped rising, dragged it back inside and unpacked the linens and blankets that had been stored with fragrant cedar chips in a chest.

Her earlier tiredness was rapidly turning to exhaustion. She could have stayed in the city overnight and faced the long neglected cottage in the morning, but she had been too anxious to return to wait. After making the bed, she checked the bubbling pot that hung over the fire. Her mind was filled with visions of how pleasurable it would be to eat a hot bowl of stew and fall into the bed, when a gigantic shadow darkened her doorway.

The kitten shot past her feet, looking panicked, all its fur standing straight up. Xanthe raised her eyebrows as she turned to watch it race into the bedroom. It disappeared under the bed.

Then she turned to the doorway where a massive dark man stood, dressed in severe black. It was the Dark Fae Queen's chief of security, Lord Tiago Black Eagle, thunderbird Wyr and forever alien in the heartland of the Dark Fae.

Surprised, she bowed to her employer. "Welcome, my lord. Please do come in."

His features were as severe as his clothing. He looked foreign to eyes that were used to the slim build, large gray eyes and pale skin of the Dark Fae, but Xanthe had since gotten used to his harsh face and imposing demeanor.

Obsidian eyes narrowed as he stared in the direction of the kitten also. "Tenanye," he said, greeting her in that abrupt way of his that no longer seemed quite so odd after her sojourn in America. "I believe I told you to stop calling me that. Tiago will do just fine. What the hell is that doing here?"

She raised her eyebrows again as he gestured to the bedroom. "The kitten?" she asked. "I found it wandering the grounds on the other side of the crossover passageway in Chicago, so I brought it with me."

The crossover passageway from Adriyel to Chicago was located on an eighty-acre tract of land just northwest of the Chicago's downtown Loop area. The grounds held a large Georgian style mansion and were bordered by a tall stone wall that was topped with rolls of barbed wire, but the front gates were made of wrought iron and since Adriyel had opened its borders, more often than not, now those gates stood open.

None of the Dark Fae staff at the mansion would adopt a companion animal, but along with giving open access to other creatures, there was more than enough opportunity for urban wildlife to take advantage of the open gates and slip into the large, wooded area.

Tiago gave her a strange look then brushed past her to stride into the bedroom. "Come out from under there," he said firmly.

Xanthe stared at him, her tired mind blank with astonishment.

The kitten slunk out from underneath the bed. It seemed even tinier and more delicate as it hunched at the Wyr lord's feet.

A wave of heat prickled Xanthe's skin as horrified comprehension began to dawn.

Tiago looked down at the small creature, hands on his hips. It stared up at him, still looking panicked, eyes completely round and fur bristling.

He ordered, "Change."

The kitten shapeshifted and became a dirty, unkempt girl who stared, seemingly mesmerized at the immense male in front of her. Tiago angled his jaw out and tilted his head at Xanthe.

Xanthe rubbed her forehead, her shoulders slumped. "Oh, gods," she said. "I kidnapped a little Wyr girl."

"She never once changed in front of you?" Tiago asked.

"No, sir. I had no idea. You know my magic sense is minimal." Xanthe had telepathy and the ability to traverse crossover passageways. She could also sense some Power in strong items and individuals, but without a Wyr's sense of smell, she hadn't any way to tell that the kitten was anything but what it seemed. She lifted her shoulders. "I thought I was rescuing a feral cat."

"Well," Tiago said after a moment. "I'll take her back to the palace with me. Niniane will know how to take care of this." He shot a look at Xanthe. "As for you, I will be in touch. I want to hear details about what happened."

"Understood, my l—sir," Xanthe said.

The little girl tore her gaze away from the towering figure in front of her to look at Xanthe. She whispered, "I want to stay here."

Immediately and in unison, Xanthe and Tiago said, "That can't happen."

"You named me Mouse," the girl said, her gaze pleading with Xanthe. "I was going to live in the cottage with you and be your mouser. You said so."

The plea tugged at Xanthe's heart. She thought of the kitten, curled on her lap and purring as she talked idly to it. She honestly could not remember all the things she had said. She walked over to squat in front of the child.

"That was when I thought you were just a cat," Xanthe told her softly. "While I would love for you to stay, I have no way to take care of a Wyr child." She had no way to take care of any child. Her life was too dangerous.

"But I like it here," the girl said plaintively. "I wouldn't be any trouble. I can be a cat all the time."

"I'm sorry, no," Xanthe said as gently as she could. She touched the girl's matted hair. "This place would not be good for you, darling. You deserve a much better place, where you can be both a cat and a little girl and go to school."

Tiago didn't wait for any more protestations. He scooped the girl up and turned toward the doorway. He said over one broad shoulder, "Relax and take some time for yourself. You've earned it. I'll send for you in the next day or two. Be ready."

"Yes, sir," Xanthe said.

Then he strode out the door. The last thing Xanthe saw of the girl were large sad eyes peering around the Wyr lord's shoulder.

Xanthe walked over to the sit at the table and rub her face. She would not reconsider as those large sad eyes had asked her to do. She could not.

Silence settled in the cottage. It seemed so much emptier than it had before Tiago had come. She stared at the items on the table that she had unloaded from her pack. There were various toiletries, weapons—her shoulder harness and sword, along with throwing knives—and the old, hand painted wooden box that held the Tarot deck.

The last of her energy had slipped away. She would put the things away tomorrow. For now, she pulled the box to her, opened it and pulled out the Tarot deck. Warm, mellow Power filled her hands as she reverently fingered the hand-painted cards.

She shuffled the deck and turned over the top card. It was one of the Major Arcana, Inanna, goddess of love, her chariot drawn by seven lions.

Inanna's card had been showing up every time she shuffled the cards.

"I thought you meant the cat," she said to the card.

The face of a golden woman smiled out at her, fierce and mysterious.

She sighed. Love came in many forms—the love of a friend or lover, a parent or child. The devotion of a pet, or the love of one's country. Xanthe was really suited for only one of those, although for a while she thought the kitten might work.

She put the deck in the box and set it gently on the fireplace mantle. Then she ate some stew and fell into bed.

The summons from the palace came early the next morning.

Everything was blanketed in light dew, and the tip of the sun barely showed through the trees. Xanthe had made a cup of tea and had taken it out to sit on an overturned log, enjoying the silence and the solitude.

It was peaceful at the cottage, with bright trills from birds and the rustle of wind blowing through the long grasses. She had never grown accustomed to the sounds and smells of American traffic, and for so long she had been unable to take much time to herself. She had always been surrounded by others she couldn't trust. It was exotic and liberating to feel the inner coil of tension that had been wound so tightly relax at last.

She heard the horseman on the path before she saw him, and the coil came back, tightening her stomach muscles. She stood and waited, and a few moments later, a palace guard trotted into view, leading another saddled, riderless horse. The guard didn't bother to dismount as he came up to her. Instead, he handed her a sealed note and the reins for the second horse, turned and left.

The note was a single word written in strong black slashes: "Come."

She blew out a breath. So much for relaxing and taking time for herself. After tethering the horse, she washed, dressed in her own palace black uniform, braided her silky hair and checked her appearance in the oval silver mirror in the bedroom.

Somewhere in the distant past, she had an ancestor who had not been Dark Fae and it showed in small ways. She was slim with an upright carriage, but her eyes were a darker gray than most Dark Fae's were. There was a sprinkle of light freckles across the bridge of her nose and along her cheeks, and her features were not quite as angular, her lips plump and curving. For those of the nobility who were concerned with the purity of breeding lines, those small differences were as good as a shout.

Not that she was likely to try to pass herself off as noble any time in the foreseeable future. She tilted her head to check that her braid was neat, then she slipped on her shoulder harness that settled her sword onto her back, spread soft cheese over a slice of bread to eat on the journey and she shut the door gently as she left the cottage.

Adriyel was not a large city by American standards, but it was beautiful and busy. Her uniform and the horse created an open path for her on the cobblestone streets as people moved to make way for her. The buildings nestled harmoniously among the trees, and there was a long waterfront park by the river near the falls. As she approached the palace, she studied it with a critical eye.

Age and simple elegance defined the palace's architecture. The building was superbly designed and proportioned, the lines deceptively simple, yet phantoms lingered in Xanthe's mind whenever she looked at it, phantoms of blood and battle and screams in the night.

Brushing them aside had long ago become habit. She took the horse to the stables and entered the palace through the servant's quarters.

The Wyr lord was in the Queen's private apartment. The two guards at the doors nodded respectfully to her and stood aside. "You're to go right in, ma'am," said the one on the right. If she remembered correctly, Rickart was his name.

"Thank you," she said. She shrugged out of her shoulder harness and handed her sword to him. One did not go armed into the Queen's presence unless expressly invited to do so.

Xanthe had only been in the Queen's apartment once before, and that had been seasons ago when the Queen and her Wyr lord had made the final decision on Xanthe's mission, so she looked around curiously as she entered. The rest of the interior of the palace was like the exterior, spacious and deceptively simple, sparely decorated with pieces of furniture, tapestries and sculptures that were national treasures.

The Queen's private apartment was another matter. In the large sitting room color was splashed everywhere. Traditional embroidered tapestries covered the walls, and bowls and vases of flowers brightened dark polished wood surfaces. Red velvet couches were arranged in front of a fireplace and piled with pillows that were also embroidered with rich gold accents. An intricately carved bowl made of some lovely, translucent green stone Xanthe wasn't familiar with held miniature Reese's peanut butter cups. A scatter of books had been left carelessly on one table. Xanthe glanced at the haphazard pile. Dark Fae books on history and politics were intermingled with American mass market paperbacks, most of them romances.

Across the room, doors had been propped open to the sunny morning. They led to the terrace that looked out over the Queen's private walled garden. Hearing male voices outside, she walked over to the doors and looked out.

The Wyr lord sat at table, chatting easily with another tall figure of a man who was, by weight of his office alone, imposing in his own right. Chancellor Aubrey Riordan was one of the triad that formed the Dark Fae government, along with the Queen and the Commander of the Dark Fae army, Fafnir Orin. The Chancellor lounged in his chair facing the morning sun as he cradled a steaming cup of tea.

There was absolutely no question of Riordan's pure Dark Fae blood. He had strong, intelligent patrician features and light gray eyes that shone like clear water in sunlight. His long raven hair was bound back in a simple queue and gleamed blue-black in the bright light, his pointed ears elegantly shaped.

In contrast to his hair, his skin was ivory pale. While he did not have the Wyr lord's outsized physique, his long lean frame was muscled with graceful power. His eyes were narrowed in the sunlight, which revealed crow's feet at their corners, and a few strands of white hair gleamed at his temples. Riordan was not a young Fae, but a male in his full maturity of Power.

As she saw him, a sweet pain like a stiletto coated in honey slipped between Xanthe's ribs and pierced her heart. It was the same pain she always felt whenever she saw him. Like a silly child with her toys, for years she had gathered the snippets she heard about his life and hoarded them close.

Servants always knew the truth about their masters' true nature. What all the servants said about Riordan was that he was kind and even tempered. He never expressed frustration with a blow or a harsh word. One of the most powerful men in Adriyel, he held onto that power lightly and used it with care. For someone like Xanthe, who had rarely known kindness, he sounded as foreign and exotic as the Wyr lord who now kept him company.

The events of the last year had been cataclysmic for the Dark Fae, and also for Riordan himself. The despot Dark Fae King Urien had been killed by Dragos Cuelebre, the Lord of the Wyr, and with his death, at first it seemed there was no clear heir to the throne. For a short time, it had been whispered that Riordan, who was a distant relative in the Lorelle line, might be crowned king.

Then Niniane Lorelle, the true heir and Urien's niece, came out of hiding. She had been living in America ever since Urien and a handful of nobles had killed her father, King Rhian, and the rest of her family in a bloody palace coup.

Riordan had been married then, to a noble woman named Naida who had not accepted Niniane's claim to the throne, and who had tried a couple of times to have her assassinated. Instead Naida herself had been killed and her coconspirators incarcerated when the plot had been uncovered.

When that had happened something light inside of Riordan had darkened. Xanthe had seen it whenever she caught a glimpse of him on the palace grounds. He looked set, withdrawn, the expression in his gaze bleak and bitter. Whenever she thought of what his wife had done, she felt a useless fury at the woman who had been a traitor and a killer, and who with her actions had wounded such a decent man.

The moment Xanthe appeared in the doorway, Tiago turned his head and so did Riordan. She dropped her gaze. "My lords."

"There you are," said Tiago. "You must have gotten my message just after dawn." He put a booted foot on one chair and pushed it outward in her direction. "Sit and eat. Niniane will join us shortly."

Disconcerted, she lowered her head. "Thank you, my l—sir. That's very good of you, but I couldn't do that."

"Oh, you Fae and your social rules," said Tiago. He sounded exasperated. "Get over yourself, soldier. Plant your ass down here and eat some breakfast. That's an order."

Startled, her head came up. Before she could help herself, she looked at Riordan.

He smiled at her, his expression warm, and gestured to the chair Tiago had pushed out from the table. "You heard your employer," said the Chancellor. "Sit and help yourself to some food."

She couldn't help but stare. He looked different somehow than he had before she had left, less bitter in repose. Perhaps time was healing the wound that his wife had dealt him.

She took a deep breath and walked over to sit gingerly. She kept her gaze on her task as she did as she was ordered and helped herself to some of the breakfast on the table. There were boiled eggs, honey and berry pastries, fresh fruit and grilled venison. The bread and cheese she had eaten earlier seemed to have vanished completely, and her stomach rumbled. She tightened the muscles in her abdomen, hoping nobody had noticed.

She started to eat, and the two men resumed talking as if she wasn't there.

"You should have mentioned something about the lawsuit sooner," Tiago said.

After a slight hesitation, Riordan said, "I disagree. It's my issue to resolve. At any rate, nothing will happen in a hurry. The suit will likely drag on for years."

Everything in Xanthe went quiet. Riordan was involved in some kind of legal dispute? It was news to her, so it must have happened while she had been away. Unwilling to show any reaction to what was obviously none of her business, she had to make a conscious decision to keep eating as she listened.

"There's no merit in the accusations," said Tiago. "You had no knowledge of what Naida was doing, and you weren't involved."

Riordan said cynically, "It doesn't matter whether or not we know that the case has any merit. The pursuant always has plenty of time to present their case and whatever they claim as true findings. That's simply how the Dark Fae justice system works. What you and Niniane achieved when you tried and executed the conspirators involved in the coup that killed her family was highly unusual, and that was because it involved the Queen herself, imprisonment of powerful nobility and high treason."

"Naida's family is claiming you were treasonous," Tiago said.

"Not quite treason, in the legal sense," said Riordan. "Niniane had not yet been crowned. The best they can hope for is a charge of conspiracy. Since I was so much older than Naida and she was so young when we married, and all of Naida's crimes were supposedly on my behalf, they're claiming that I exerted 'undue influence' over her. Anyway, as you know only the government can instigate criminal cases. Since this is a personal suit and not an affair of the crown, the only thing they can hope to gain is monetary compensation."

"So they're being greedy," said Tiago after a moment.

"Yes," said Riordan flatly. "And to be brutally fair, they're also angry and they've suffered a loss, not only in terms of family but also their reputation."

"Well, the person they should be angry with is dead, and there isn't any evidence you had anything to do with it. I had you investigated myself."

"Of course you did," said Riordan. "I would have had me investigated as well."

Xanthe swallowed carefully, the food threatening to lodge in her throat. As she hadn't been involved in any investigating, that was more news to her. But as she considered it, she couldn't say she was surprised.

The Queen meant the world to the Wyr lord, and he was one of the most dangerous men she had ever met. He would have left no stone unturned in his investigation of Riordan. Even if he had not found any evidence, if he had the slightest suspicion that Riordan might have been involved in something that could potentially harm the Queen, Riordan was a dead man.

Having just killed a man herself on the Wyr lord's orders, she should know.

Chapter Two

Law

At first the silent woman in the soldier's uniform hadn't interested Aubrey, other than he took note of how openly Tiago talked in front of her. Although Tiago and Niniane never flaunted anything in public, they were a love match. The Wyr was obsessed with anything to do with his mate, and her safety and wellbeing. If Tiago relaxed and talked in front of this woman, then Aubrey could too.

Gradually, though, the woman's very silence drew Aubrey's attention. He glanced at her from time to time, noting various details, how precisely and smoothly she cut her food, the utter expressionlessness in her face, how she never looked up once from her meal. She embodied polite distance, her entire demeanor proclaiming that an invisible wall existed between her and the two men.

A patter of quick, light footsteps sounded on the terrace flagstones, and Tiago's harsh, forbidding features lit up. The woman shot to her feet and stood at attention. Aubrey and Tiago stood at a more leisurely pace as Niniane Lorelle, the Dark Fae Queen swept into their presence, chatting as she came toward them.

"Sorry I am late—oh good, you didn't wait for me. Good morning, Aubrey."

"Good morning, my dear." He bent his head to receive Niniane's kiss on the cheek.

She was dressed for personal comfort rather than for state, in simple dark tunic and leggings. She was dainty in every way, and while she wasn't precisely beautiful, she had a warmth and effervescence that could always banish the darkness in Aubrey's soul, at least for a while. She was the child of his long dead friends, and the only Lorelle left alive, and he had grown to love her like he would if she were his own daughter.

Still talking, she moved around the table to Tiago. "Hello, darling." Niniane lifted her face for Tiago's kiss, which he delivered to her mouth with relish. "I've just come from the nursery. I wanted to check on the girl. She is adorable, but she still won't say anything about where she came from or who she really is, and she insists that her name is Mouse."

"At least she's talking to you and the nurse," said Tiago. "She wouldn't say a word to me. I frightened her too much."

Niniane gave him a wry grimace. "The nearest I can tell, she has got to be around six years old. Given how ingrained the dirt was on her, and how matted her hair, I think it's possible she might have lived on the streets for some time. If that's the case, I think she might have changed into her cat form and stayed that way to survive.

I sent someone this morning to Chicago to do some investigating. For all we know, there might be pictures of her on milk cartons." Her expression turned troubled. "I suppose we shouldn't keep her, should we?"

Tiago shook his head, his face gentling. "No, faerie. It would not be fair to a young Wyr to be fostered among the Dark Fae. Housecat Wyr have life spans akin to humans. That would not matter at first, but eventually she would grow old while everyone she grew to care about would not. She needs a good home with her own kind."

Niniane's shoulders drooped. "I knew that," she muttered. "I just needed to hear you say it to me."

As the two talked, Aubrey glanced at the soldier again. Hands tucked behind her back, she regarded her half eaten plate of food as though it was the only thing in the world of interest to her. A corner of Aubrey's mouth lifted. She was really quite good.

"Sit down," said Tiago. "I'll order fresh tea and hot food for you."

"No, don't bother," said Niniane. "This is all fine." She turned to face the silent woman with a friendly grin. "So you're the one who kidnapped a little Wyr girl?"

The woman's façade broke. She moved, looked up and took in a deep breath as color flooded her skin, and after such a long display of perfect, polite disinterest, the look of dismay on her face startled a quiet chuckle out of Aubrey.

"Yes, your grace, I am," said the woman. "I am terribly sorry."

She looked more than sorry; she looked so mortified even Tiago grinned.

"Don't be," said Niniane. "Your 'kidnapping' might have saved her life." She sat and helped herself to breakfast while Tiago poured her a cup of tea. "What have I missed?"

Aubrey and Tiago sat too. The woman remained standing until Tiago shot her a frowning glance. Then she sat as well, although she did not touch any more of her food. Tiago said, "Aubrey and I were discussing a suit that Naida's family has filed against him."

"Yes, I learned of it this morning when my secretary briefed me," said the Queen, her voice turning cool. "I have already sent a dismissal to Justice Kellen for the court."

The woman's reactions, or lack of, had begun to fascinate Aubrey, so he was looking at her when Niniane spoke. He watched a subtle, strange expression flare in her dark gray eyes. Oddly, it appeared to be relief mingled with satisfaction, but he must be mistaken. Then the meaning of Niniane's words caught up with him, and he set his cup down gently as he turned to the Queen.

The monarchy had every right to dismiss cases and issue pardons, but in actuality this was done so rarely that the action carried a great deal of weight. The dismissal would be highly public by the end of the day and a great humiliation to Naida's family.

He said, "While I am both touched and honored by your show of faith, I had thought Naida's family's anger might run its course during the length of the suit."

Tiago said, much more bluntly, "Are you sure you want to do that, faerie?"

"Yes, I am quite sure," said Niniane. She snapped a delicate bite of food off of her fork then pointed her fork at Aubrey. "You are Chancellor by my appointment. Naida's attempt was on my life, and I assure you, we investigated that quite thoroughly. For months that was almost the only thing Tiago and I talked about, along with the investigation of Urien's conspirators."

"I can attest to that," Tiago said.

Niniane stabbed her fork in the air, eyes sparking with anger. "At best their case against you would have been full of supposition and resentment, and at worst, full of fabrication. That suit was not just a slap in the face to you, Aubrey. It was a slap in the face to me. I will not have my people harassed. I will not have my judgments questioned like that. The dismissal is the best thing that could have happened for them, because if they were allowed to continue and if they were foolish enough to present false evidence, I would order the courts to prosecute them. If they think their lives are ruined now, it would be nothing compared to what would happen to them then."

Silence fell over the table. Tiago's expression was filled with, yes, amusement and indulgence, but also genuine admiration and respect. The woman who was his soldier watched the Queen with sparkling eyes, while Niniane continued to point her fork at Aubrey, eyebrows raised.

Aubrey cleared his throat. "Since you put it that way, thank you for your championship."

She smiled at him. "You're welcome. Now, onto something else." She looked at the soldier sitting opposite her. "Your name is Xanthe, is that correct? Tiago tells me you have a tale to tell."

Aubrey watched the woman glance at him then at Tiago, who nodded. "Speak freely," he told her.

She nodded and took a breath. "My assignment has been completed. Cieran Thruvial is dead. He died in a place called Devil's Gate in Nevada, where we went after we had crossed over to America."

The place name was unfamiliar to Aubrey but he wasn't surprised at that. He watched as Niniane and Tiago gave each other a long look.

Tiago murmured, "It's finally done. The last of them have been brought to justice."

"We can look to the future now," Niniane said. They shared an intimate smile. Then Niniane turned back to Xanthe. "I've never heard of this place."

"Devil's Gate is new since your grace has come to Adriyel," said Xanthe. "A—a tent city, they call it, although many of the structures are not tents. Some are vehicles called RVs. Others are buildings they called Quonset and there are also temporary office spaces made of metal. Close to two hundred thousand people, both humankind and Elder Races, are there now looking for magic sensitive silver and gold."

"There's a modern day gold rush going on, and I didn't know anything about it?" Niniane sounded dismayed.

"You need more sleep than I do," Tiago said to her. "I've been following the stories in the newspapers."

Niniane muttered, "We have got to start spending some time each year in Chicago, especially now that we've opened our borders."

"Agreed," said Tiago. He told Xanthe, "Continue."

She said, "The place is—crowded and chaotic. Lord Thruvial thought he could relax in some relative anonymity there. He was well away from Adriyel's politics and the trials of all the other conspirators. He believed that since you could not find enough evidence of his involvement in the overthrow and murder of your father and family that he would not be pursued further."

Aubrey looked steadily across the table at the deadly face of the man who sat opposite him. Thruvial had not only been a pig, but an idiot.

Xanthe said, "Since I was the most junior of his triad, for a long time I was not allowed to perform any of the more intimate tasks of service to him, like serving him food and drink or helping him to dress."

"She was in his household for months," Tiago told Aubrey. "It never fails to surprise me how assholes like Thruvial insist on Dark Fae traditions like keeping triads of personal servants, but then they can turn around and murder their own king."

Triads were found throughout all aspects of the Dark Fae daily life, from the highest place in government to fighting formations and servant clusters. Often in society, married couples brought a third sex partner to the marriage bed, although Aubrey had never felt inclined to do so.

He gave Tiago a dark smile. "That is not inconsistent, my friend. Our traditions of violence, jealousy, revenge, and making and breaking political alliances, go deeper than any triad."

Tiago snorted. "Point." He said to Xanthe, "So Thruvial finally relaxed and let you get close enough."

"Yes, but even so, I had to wait for the right moment to act so that it could not be traced back to me. When the opportunity finally came, I poisoned his wine." Her voice was composed and steady. "He died quickly. Unfortunately that was not the end of it."

Aubrey settled back in his chair, watching her face as she told the story. There were odd, intriguing freckles, light like sprinkles of gold, on her nose and cheeks. Her eyes were unusual too, a deep, rich color full of shadows and mystery. Her face was gently planed, with high cheekbones and a narrow rounded jaw. Now that he came to really study her, he realized she had a shockingly sensual mouth. She would never be considered one of the high beauties of the Dark Fae, but she did have her own particular attractiveness.

"There was trouble?" Tiago asked.

"Yes. A young medusa also resided in Devil's Gate, and she was known to argue publicly with Lord Thruvial. When his other attendants found him poisoned, they started an outcry that ran through the camp. They insisted that she was the one who poisoned him, and she was taken and locked up to be hung." Her expression turned bitter. "The whole thing was entirely my fault. I did not consider all the ramifications of what might happen if I killed him in such a fashion. I simply saw my opportunity and took it."

Niniane leaned forward. "You can't consider how everybody might react to something. It's too much to ask of yourself."

Other than a quick glance at the Queen, Aubrey's gaze returned to Xanthe's face. He was interested to note that her self-recriminating expression hadn't changed even though the Queen herself offered absolution. This young soldier had a strong set of scruples.

He asked in a quiet voice, "Is the medusa girl all right?"

She turned to him quickly. "Yes, my lord. While I waited and watched for an opportunity to help, her aunt and a friend came. Together we were all able to get out." She looked at Tiago and Niniane. "You actually know them—it was Duncan Turner and Dr. Seremela Telemar."

Aubrey was acquainted with Duncan slightly, for he had met the young Vampyre when Niniane had travelled from Chicago to Adriyel for her coronation. Niniane had been accompanied by a Dark Fae delegation, along with the Vampyre Carling Severan, who had been a member of the Elder tribunal, and her attendants. Aubrey didn't know the physician, but it was clear from Tiago and

Niniane's intense startlement that they knew both of the others.

"You already said that everybody is all right, but how are Duncan and Seremela?" Niniane asked. She sounded wistful. "I would love to see them again."

"They were quite well when I took my leave," Xanthe told her. "And so was Dr. Telemar's niece. They said to offer you their very best wishes."

Tiago nodded to her in approval. "Despite your misgivings, it sounds like all ended well."

She hesitated. "That's not all, sir."

Aubrey set his cup down as Tiago's eyes narrowed. "What is it?"

She straightened her knife in precise alignment with her fork, gaze focused on her hand, as she said, "Lord Thruvial's other two attendants caught up with us before we could get clear away. Duncan Turner and I had to kill them. The fight was not quiet, and there may have been witnesses. Before that point, I had declared publicly that I was in support of the young medusa's innocence." This time when she lifted her gaze, her expression was resigned. "I'm the only surviving member from Thruvial's household, and I disappeared right after his attendants were killed. For any particularly clever observer, it would not be hard to put two and two together, and there were any number of clever people at Devil's Gate. With information now flowing freely from America into Adriyel..." She let her voice trail away into silence.

Tiago folded his arms as he regarded her. "Your identity has been compromised. I cannot use you for other undercover assignments."

Xanthe's shoulders slumped. Even though she had been the one to bring the point up, Aubrey could see how clearly Tiago's words disappointed her. Something about it moved him. Loyalty and dedication were precious things, and hers showed in her eyes, shining straight like a sword.

He heard himself saying, "Do not distress yourself over this. Your service will not go unrewarded. You are too valuable of an asset to waste."

This time when she looked at him, she did not glance quickly and away. Instead she met and held his gaze. He found himself looking at her deeply. He did not know what he saw in her eyes—surprise? Gratitude? He did not know her well enough to read the nuances.

"I like her," Niniane said suddenly. Her voice broke the unexpected connection that had grown between them, and they both turned to her. The Queen rested her chin in one hand as she studied Xanthe. "She's discreet, she rescues kittens and she cares about the consequences of her actions." She said to Tiago, "I want her."

His expression turned indulgent. "If you want her, you can have her."

"Well, thank you," Niniane said, "but I think we should consult with her about that." She turned back to Xanthe. "What do you think? Would you like to come work with me as one of my attendants? Please answer truthfully. I know guard duty isn't for everyone, and those who have been close to me in the last year have not fared very well." A shadow darkened her eyes, and Aubrey remembered the casualties from last year, a bright human woman named Cameron Rogers who died while saving Niniane's life, and Arethusa, the late Commander of the Dark Fae army.

As he thought of them, his heart felt as heavy as a stone, and as dead. So many deaths, so much grief, that Naida had caused.

Niniane shook herself visibly and continued. "Perhaps you are no longer interested in active duty or this position, so you won't hurt my feelings if you would rather not. We will make sure that you are placed in a position to which you are suited and that will make you happy."

Pleasure had lit Xanthe's expression, and in that moment she was truly beautiful. "I'm deeply honored, your grace, and I would love to work for you."

The shadows disappeared from Niniane's gaze, and she clapped her hands. "Oh goody!"

"I promised her time off first," Tiago said. "She's earned it."

"Of course she has," Niniane said. She asked Xanthe, "How much time would you like?"

"Might I take a sevenday?" the other woman asked in a diffident tone.

"You have been gone for some time. You may take a month—I mean a moon—if you like," Niniane told her. "Are you sure a sevenday is sufficient?"

Xanthe nodded.

"Very well, come to me first thing on the eighth day." Niniane gestured to Xanthe's unfinished plate of food. "Have you had all that you want?"

"Yes, your grace."

"Then your vacation begins now. Thank you for telling us what happened, and enjoy your sevenday."

Xanthe stood, bowed deeply to Niniane, inclined her head at Tiago and Aubrey, and left.

Silence fell over the three who remained on the terrace, as Niniane resumed work on her breakfast and Tiago sank deep into his thoughts.

Aubrey finished his tea, his own thoughts turning dark as they always did anymore when he looked inward. He suspected that the most interesting part of his day had just taken her leave.

After Niniane finished her meal, she turned her attention to him and began asking questions. He had breakfast with Niniane a few times every sevenday, so that he could keep her abreast of the latest happenings in the congress and the courts. Sometimes Tiago joined them, and sometimes he didn't. After listening to their conversation for several minutes, Tiago excused himself.

The rest of Aubrey's schedule was filled with the never ending administrative part of his duties as Chancellor. He found himself wondering what the young soldier, Xanthe, was doing with the first of her sevenday, and how she was enjoying her time off. While she must have been around before on the extensive palace grounds, she would have been virtually anonymous among all of the black uniformed guards, and he had never noticed her before.

What would that quiet, reserved woman do for pleasure? Did she read, or work with metal, or garden or paint? After having been gone for so long, she must feel quite out of touch with her friends, if she had any. It was hard to maintain friendships when one worked as an agent for the crown.

As the afternoon faded to evening, his thoughts turned to Naida's family. The Ealdun family were minor nobility and much poorer than Aubrey. Naida's marriage to Aubrey had been advantageous to them in every way, and now they had not only lost that connection by marriage, but their daughter had been branded a traitor.

Aubrey hadn't minded either the social and financial differences, or the age difference, as Naida had been much younger than he. He had not loved Naida the way that Niniane and Tiago loved each other. He couldn't remember if he had ever hoped to find that kind of fierce, passionate love. If he had, it was lost in the distance of his long ago youth.

But he had known long, deeply caring liaisons with many lovers, and he had enjoyed his marriage with Naida, enjoyed having her companionship in the daytime hours and in bed. She had been clever, strong minded, and quick to grasp political and social nuances, and she had been funny, her wit dry and often sardonic. He had loved and respected her, and had considered her a good partner and a friend.

He had trusted her.

What she had done had come as a raw shock. Her attempts to kill Niniane were not only a betrayal of the true heir, but most importantly, they were a betrayal of him. What she had done went against everything that Aubrey stood for and believed in, and if she had succeeded in killing Niniane, he knew that she would have never told him what she had done.

In the aftermath of her death, he doubted himself and his own judgment of people. He might have missed her, except when the shock and guilt eased enough for other feelings to come in, he felt so angry at her for what she had done. He wanted to shout at her and throw her out of house, and he could do none of that of because she was dead.

He had no idea how he would ever grow to trust someone again. He felt so angry all of the time, and bitter. He felt cheated. He understood how the Ealduns might feel angry and cheated too.

How would they react to the news of the Queen's dismissal? He believed they would take it very badly and he braced himself for the possibility of ugly missives awaiting him when he arrived home, or even a confrontation in public or possible retaliation in another way.

They had already dropped out of social gatherings, and it would be some years before their reputation recovered enough for them to receive invitations again. Prosecuting him had been, among other things, a way for them to try to distance themselves from the stain of what Naida had done. They could have claimed horror and righteous indignation, and they must have hoped to turn censure away by pointing fingers at someone else, but now that avenue had been denied them.

He also understood Niniane's anger and the reasons for her dismissal of the Ealdun's lawsuit, but he could not help but wish it had been allowed to run its course.

For one thing, he had been most interested to find out what evidence the Ealdun s might offer up to the court as proof of his undue influence over Naida.

He had wanted to know just how far they would go for money, and for their pride.

Perhaps he could still find out. He sent for one of his junior secretaries, a steady, discreet fellow named Sebrin who had a very sharp mind. Once Sebrin had stepped inside his office, he nodded for the younger male to shut the door.

"You might have heard the news by now," he said. "The Queen has dismissed the Ealduns' lawsuit against me."

"Oh, very good, sir," said Sebrin, which did not happen to confirm whether he had heard already or not.

Aubrey suppressed a smile. Discreet, indeed. He was pleased with his choice in hiring Sebrin. He said, "I want you to dig quietly into the details of that lawsuit. See if you discover what sort of evidence they claimed to have. I don't expect they would have had time to file anything detailed, so this will probably not be in court records. You may have to travel to the Ealdun's home seat." He paused. "Do you understand what I am asking you to do?"

He could see in the other man's intelligent expression that Sebrin understood him perfectly. "Yes, my lord."

"Do you have any problem with the assignment?"

"Not at all, my lord." Sebrin added emphasis to each word, his eyes sparkling. "I think it will be quite interesting."

"Very good. Be careful and keep your head down. That will be all." He sat back in his chair, his hands steepled together as he watched Sebrin bow and take his leave.

He wasn't sure what he would do with the answers when he received them, but it still felt good to take at least some kind of action. He hoped he would be wrong, but he fully expected to be incensed at whatever Sebrin might find. After all, the Ealduns would not have filed a lawsuit if they hadn't believed they could argue a case against him.

In the meantime, he would get nothing else accomplished at work that day. As the sun dipped below the horizon, he finally sent his secretaries off. Then as was his habit, he walked the short distance along torch lit streets to the stylish neighborhood near the palace where his house was located.

It was an old and gracious building, and despite the triads of servants it held to fulfill his every whim, somehow it was still quite empty.

Chapter Three

Death

"I t's the Queen, isn't it?" Xanthe asked Inanna's card that night.

The love of one's country could certainly be personified as the love of one's Queen. This possibility fit even better than the kitten had.

The card, of course, made no comment. Divination came through Elder Tarot decks in ways other than outright language, depending on which card spread one laid. All the Major Arcana were the seven Elder gods, the primal Powers that moved and sustained the universe. Love, Death, Will, Law, The Depths, The Hearth. And the god who was god over all the others, The Dance.

All the Minor Arcana were the various aspects of each god. The nuances were in the combinations. Love and Death could mean grief or loss. Love and Will, which was sometimes known as The Gift, could mean sacrifice. The most accurate and comprehensive messages were found in a complete spread.

At least, that was true of a normal Tarot deck.

When she had traveled back from Devil's Gate to Chicago with Duncan Turner, Seremela Telemar and her niece, Xanthe had cheated.

Because Seremela was a physician with highly trained magical skills, the others had assumed that she was the expert when she examined the mysterious Tarot deck that her niece had stolen. And she was, mostly. All Xanthe had to do was remain silent while she watched and listened. She learned that despite Seremela's expertise, the physician couldn't identify what kind of Power infused the cards, or what the Power might mean, or how it might exert influence on the world around it.

Xanthe never told them that she knew how to lay a Tarot spread. She also never told them of the tiny suspicion that had been born as she listened to Seremela speculate. She simply took the opportunity to gain possession of the cards when it presented itself.

The others expected her to take the deck to Dark Fae elders and experts.

She might do that, eventually.

There were ancient shrines dotted throughout Adriyel, dedicated to each of the Elder gods. She might also take the deck to each of the shrines to see if something happened, although she had not decided about that. For now Seremela had said the Power in the deck had pulled to Xanthe, and so she honored the deck's wishes by keeping it.

The oldest of the old Dark Fae legends spoke of Powerful things that existed, put into the world by the gods to enact their will. If this was such an incredibly rare item, and if Xanthe had the knowledge, Power and skill with which to use it, she could come to rule the Dark Fae if she so wished.

If and if. For all their vast power, the gods could not take away a person's free will, and Xanthe did not so wish. Nor did she have the knowledge, Power or skill. She hadn't even gotten up the courage to actually lay out a complete spread, although she would one day soon.

For now she held the cards and shuffled them. She enjoyed the gentle, mellow feel of the Power that soaked into her hands as she handled them, and she liked to study the lovely hand-painted images while quiet whispers and vague images brushed along the edges of her mind.

And she took sober, respectful note of how Inanna's card continued to surface.

Part of why she lacked the courage to lay a complete spread was she did not want to witness an augury that was filled with sacrifice or grief. Instead, she liked to imagine that Inanna's card meant good things, light things.

Her long trip from home had been dark and violent. She had witnessed Thruvial and the others do things that turned her stomach and sickened her soul, and she had to do all of that with more than just an expressionless face. If she could not manage enjoyment, she had to at least feign support. She had not known from day to day if she would even survive the trip. There had been many nights when she would lie awake and wonder if she would die alone without friends.

Now, even if it was only for a little while, she needed to imagine those good, light things.

"You would not deny me that, would you?" she asked Inanna.

The woman on the card. She was so strong, so strong.

Xanthe spent her sevenday working on the cottage, cutting and weeding away the long tangled foliage, arranging for wood to be delivered, and walking the short path to sit and dream by the Adriyel River. Sometimes she fished for her supper. Sometimes she waded in the shallows at the edge of the river where she had played as a child.

Sometimes she watched the river barges until the sun dropped low and shone a shimmering path on the dappled, mysterious surface, beckoning her to walk an impossible journey on the water into the light.

She spoke to as few people as possible and let the silence sink into her soul. It washed away some of the terrible stains, not all, but enough so that she did not lie awake at night, dwelling on thoughts of her own death.

On the eighth day, first thing in the morning, she presented herself at the palace to await the Queen's pleasure.

The Queen was very pleased indeed.

"Whee!" said Niniane, grinning widely as Xanthe stepped into her apartment. "There you are! I'm so excited that you are here. Did you have a good time on your vacation? Did you get enough rest? I will be most unhappy if you ever try to fib to me because it is something you think I want to hear."

"I have rested quite well, thank you, your grace. I am excited and honored to be here."

Xanthe stood at rest, her hands clasped loosely behind her back as she regarded the smaller woman with some bemusement. Niniane was dressed in a pale pink, filmy wraparound robe that had a neckline and hem of floating, tiny feathers. She wore odd, dainty American shoes that matched, with high heels and a single strap that somehow held them onto her feet, and with more of the floating, tiny pink feathers along the strap. Her dark hair was pinned up, and somehow it looked both messy and softly feminine.

Niniane caught the direction of her gaze and held out a small foot. "This ridiculous floaty, feathery stuff is marabou, and I love it beyond all reason."

"It is certainly striking," Xanthe told her in perfect truthfulness.

The Queen giggled. "How precisely worded of you. You know, I am quite the proper Dark Fae Queen out there." She waved her hands in the general direction of the doors. "But in here, in private, I get to relax and be anything I want to be. The only thing is—" She looked around mournfully. "I don't have cable."

Xanthe blinked. "Then I shall fetch one for you immediately. It would help for me to know what kind of cable you require."

Niniane giggled harder. "Oh no, I do not require that kind of cable. 'Cable' is slang for cable TV. I suppose in

Thruvial's household, you did not have access to any television during your months in America?"

"Ah, no," said Xanthe. "However, we were able to examine a television in one of the motels we stayed in when we journeyed to Nevada." She paused then added delicately, "Watching this device seemed an odd pastime."

"Oh, it is," Niniane assured her. "It's also fun, if there is a good story to watch. Theoretically. In Cuelebre Tower in New York, the cable company was horrendous and installed everything wrong. Then they couldn't seem to get it fixed right until Dragos himself went to talk to the head of the company. After that, the problems were fixed within a week. All eighty floors." She heaved a sigh. "It must be good to be a dragon."

"One imagines so," said Xanthe politely.

She settled quickly into her new routine and duties, which were at times not at all what she had expected. The Queen had lived for two hundred years in New York, and while, as she had said, she maintained formality in public, in private she indulged in her odd, casual American ways. Often she and Tiago dined privately in her apartment. On the occasional nights when the Queen was not engaged, yet Tiago was away at work, Xanthe learned how to play card games called euchre and hearts, and once she endured a painfully long board game called Monopoly. She was not eager to repeat the experience.

She found that while she had taken her sevenday, investigators had discovered that the little Wyr girl's mother was a drug addict who was so far gone in her own mind, she hadn't noticed the child had been missing. The investigators had contacted other family members who, shocked to find out what had happened, had filed for emergency custody. As soon as they could arrange to do so, they would be traveling to Adriyel to collect the girl and bring her home. Niniane would provide financial help so that they could take time away from their jobs and make the journey. Xanthe was sorry to hear of the mother's neglect, but glad to know the child would go to a home where she would be cared for and she could belong.

On the days when she had early duty, afterward she traveled home to the cottage. When she had late duty, she stayed overnight in the palace barracks. Every sevenday she received her wages and she got not one but two full days off, a new policy which had been instituted by this Americanized Queen and felt like the height of luxury. She also received several moons pay that was owed to her for her assignment to infiltrate Thruvial's household and execute Tiago's kill order. For the first time in a very long time, she had a tidy nest egg that she could set aside and leave untouched.

On the one hand it felt good wear the palace black, not to have to cover up her identity or put on a mask. On the other hand, there were times when the guard duty felt too passive. Fortunately the Queen was quite active. Due to Xanthe's senior status, she could have become captain of the Queen's personal guard, but that would have involved extra boring duties such as scheduling, and besides, Rickart was a good man and didn't deserve to be supplanted.

She saw Chancellor Riordan often, as much as several times a week. He and the Queen might take a walk through the palace grounds as they discussed an issue, or they shared breakfast. They often attended the same functions, whether it was a dinner of state, or some gala like the annual regatta, where boats and barges of all sizes and kinds floated on the river, lit with colored lanterns that reflected off the sparkling black water until the night was ablaze with light. During those occasions, Xanthe usually saw Riordan from a distance, although there were always the moments when he greeted Niniane. Then he would glance at Xanthe and smile.

She treasured those smiles. They were fleeting, and of course they meant nothing. They were just a courtesy, little more than a pat one might give a horse. But he looked right into her eyes when he smiled, and for the briefest moment, she felt outside of her life, transported somewhere else.

She had already devoted herself to the Queen when she went to work for Tiago. It was easy to grow fond of Niniane, who was funny, charming and kind to everybody, including her servants. But Xanthe would have taken the position as Queen's attendant solely for the chance of receiving one of those rare smiles from Riordan.

One night soon after the regatta, Niniane had just finished a dinner in the great hall with prominent American businessmen and a collective of Dark Fae artisans and metalworkers. Neither Riordan nor Tiago had attended. The palace was built on a hillside, and the great hall was on the lower level with massive windows that offered a spectacular view of the nearby falls and river.

The Americans were suitably impressed, and the Dark Fae artisans were frankly delighted. The results looked to be highly promising for a healthy increase in trade, but the affair had gone on overlong, and Xanthe was hot, tired and hungry. She had eaten a snack just before the dinner and a full meal would be waiting for her in the kitchen, but she was just as inclined to slap a piece of meat between two pieces of bread, go to her bed in the barrack and call an end to the day.

Niniane looked as tired as she felt. She gestured for one of the servers who came to her immediately. "Please let Lord Black Eagle know that the dinner is over, and I am retiring for the night."

"Yes, your grace." The server trotted away.

Niniane glanced at Xanthe and gave a ghost of a chuckle. "I enjoy dinners like this, but there's a limit to how many functions poor Tiago can endure, so I try not to ask too much of him."

Xanthe inclined her head. Also, she thought, the risk factor for this dinner had not been high. There was a distinct pattern to the lord's behavior. Anything to do with Dark Fae nobility or involving open air, like the regatta, and Tiago was sure to attend. He was also present for anything that Niniane particularly loved, such as going to a drama house to see any of the many plays that were dark, twisting tales filled with swordfights, deceit, treachery and impossible love. "Bloody soap operas," he called them, but he said it in that easygoing indulgent way of his that seemed for Niniane alone, and besides, Xanthe suspected that he enjoyed the plays too.

She and Niniane walked back to the Queen's apartment. They had climbed the grand staircase to the upper hall when she heard running footsteps behind them. All the blood in her body pounded. She shoved Niniane forward and drew her sword as she spun to meet the newcomer, because running at that urgent pace in the palace was never good.

She recognized the palace runner immediately and straightened out of attack position, although she did not sheathe her sword. The runner, a young girl named Drinde and unarmed, paused cautiously several steps below Xanthe and held onto the guard rail, gasping for breath. "Pardon, ma'am—your Highness. Oh, you must come quickly!"

Niniane had come up beside Xanthe, her face blanched white. In a harsh voice that sounded quite unlike her, she snapped, "What has happened?"

"It's Chancellor Riordan, your grace," Drinde stammered. "He has been attacked. His servants—his servants say it is very bad."

Xanthe's world gave an ugly, sickening lurch. Beside her, Niniane tore off the stiff, richly worked, knee length jacket she wore. The jacket was a work of art and highly restrictive. She threw it to the floor. Underneath it she wore a thin shirt made of fine cotton, leggings and polished ankle boots.

"Let's go," Niniane said.

Abruptly Xanthe's mind clicked over to icy logic that won control just barely over the hot panic galloping through her body. "We don't know the veracity of this. It might be a trap." She turned to Drinde. "Are you sure they were the Chancellor's servants?"

The girl met her gaze. "Yes, ma'am."

That meant nothing. It could still be a trap. Everything inside of her was screaming to race to Riordan's house. Instead, she forced herself to say to Niniane, "I have to advise you to wait until Tiago is found."

"Noted," the Queen said in a clipped tone. "We're not waiting. We'll collect guards on our way out." The Queen looked at Drinde. "Find Lord Black Eagle. Tell him what has happened, and where we have gone."

Niniane didn't wait to hear the girl's reply. She turned and raced down the hall, and Xanthe raced beside her. They burst through a set of doors, out into a warm, humid night. Xanthe shouted for guards and several came running. She asked Niniane, "A carriage?"

"It's quicker on foot," Niniane said. Her eyes were frightened and bleak.

Xanthe rapped out orders. The guards surrounded Niniane, and they all took off running, down the colonnade of ancient sycamores, along the stately mansions on Ambassador's Row, cutting across a small park and then racing down that street to the end where the Chancellor's house was ablaze with torchlight. All the while Xanthe remained at a razor's edge, just this side of violence, her gaze darting around to every dark shadow and to the guards that surrounded her and the Queen, while her mind kept replaying those few, terrible words that Drinde had spoken.

"*He has been attacked.*"

Riordan was strong, and he would have access to some of the most highly skilled and Powerful physicians in Adriyel.

If the physicians could reach him in time.

"*His servants say it is very bad.*"

One of their guards raised his fist to pound at the front door of the Chancellor's house, just as it opened. A distressed male servant looked out at them. His gaze landed on Niniane, and his face crumpled. "Your Majesty, this is so terrible—"

Niniane said through whitened lips, "Is he dead?"

"No, not—no." The male stood back, holding the door open wide, and Niniane would have raced into the house, except Xanthe grabbed her arm and stopped her.

"You and you," Xanthe said, pointing to two of the guards. "Come inside with us. The rest of you, check the perimeter of the house. Guard all exit points, doors and windows." She released Niniane's arm and ran into the house with her, followed by the two guards.

The interior was a blur of rich wood furniture and golden, glowing lamps. Riordan's major domo led them up the stairs to where several servants stood, weeping. Xanthe's stomach was tight with raw nerves. She and Niniane looked through the open doors of an apartment.

Inside was an expansive, elegantly masculine bedroom, the hangings to a large bed pulled back. Two
people, a male and a female, were working over a lax,
bloody body. Power surged and eddied around the three
of them. Xanthe clenched her teeth as nausea welled, her
body rebelling at the sight. As quickly as it hit, it passed,
leaving a sheen of cold sweat on her hands and face.

"If you've come to gawk, get out," said the male
without looking up. "I won't have his lordship subjected
to it."

"I'm not here to gawk," Niniane said shortly.

The man's head jerked around. "Your Majesty—my
profound apologies—"

"Forget about it. Focus on your patient. Is he—will
he—?" Niniane's voice stopped abruptly as she clenched
a fist in Xanthe's uniform sleeve.

The physician turned back to his patient. He said
tersely, "I don't know. With respect, please leave us to
work now."

"Yes, of course," Niniane whispered.

Xanthe put an arm around the smaller woman's
shoulders, hugging Niniane tightly against her side. She
did not know if she did so for Niniane or for herself. She
could not look away from the man on the bed. His bare,
well formed chest was mottled with sword gashes. A
blackened bruise disfigured fully half of his still face, and
oh gods, all that blood.

Xanthe had seen such terrible wounds before. Most
of those who had suffered them had died. Riordan
disappeared in a wet haze as her eyes filled. She cleared

her throat and said huskily, "Come, let's find a sitting room."

"Of course," Niniane whispered again.

Riordan's major domo had just shown them to a sitting room when Tiago blazed into the house. It took some effort to endure the Wyr lord's presence when he was in a rage. Xanthe retreated as Tiago enfolded Niniane in his arms and asked her questions filled with quiet urgency.

Xanthe stepped out into the hall and looked for the major domo. When she found him, she asked, "How did it happen?"

He looked at her with red rimmed eyes. "We don't know, ma'am. The Chancellor was late. Well, he almost always works late these days. Tonight he was later than usual. He always tells us, you see, whenever he has an engagement or is detained. He's a thoughtful lord, a good lord."

"I know he is," she whispered.

"But he didn't come, and he didn't send word. Finally I sent two servants to look for him. They found him in the park like this. It was clear he had fought. There was blood everywhere. I sent for the physicians then to the palace."

Rage whipped through Xanthe, its sting as harsh as a cat-o-nine tail. "Why did he not have guards with him?"

The major domo blinked rapidly. "It was not his way. He said it was such a short walk from the palace grounds to his doorstep, he felt stupid calling for a guard every time he made the journey."

She pulled herself up short. The major domo did not deserve her rage. The people who attacked Riordan did. She nodded to him and left him with a quiet word of thanks, returning to wait with Niniane and Tiago in the sitting room. They didn't seem to mind when she reappeared, but she went to the window anyway and pretended to stand guard there.

The dark hours trickled by and turned to the bleak gray before dawn when the major domo stepped into the open doorway. "The physicians ask that you come," he said.

Niniane and Tiago rushed out of the room and raced up the stairs, with Xanthe close behind. She followed them into the bedroom and closed the door behind her on the anxious faces awaiting in the hall. Her hands shook. Any moment now, she thought, I will be sent out to wait with the others.

But no one seemed to notice or care that she was in the room. The physicians didn't know who she was, and Tiago and Niniane paid no attention to what she did. They were both focused on the man and woman who were tiredly washing up at basins that had been placed on a nearby sideboard.

"He'll live," the woman told them. "But he almost didn't. I was certain a couple of times that his spirit had left his body." She looked at them. "His injuries were severe and extensive, and we did the best we could but there's only so much we can do. It may take several hours to a day for him to regain consciousness, and he'll need to convalesce in peace and quiet. No work and no stress, not for a few sevendays at the very least. He's a strong man, and he used a lot of that to survive. Now he'll need to rebuild that strength."

Xanthe did not truly hear anything past the first two words. As both Tiago and Niniane asked questions and the doctors answered, she slipped like a ghost around all of them and approached the unconscious man on the bed.

She was an expert at murder, and this was how murder was done—by gaining the trust of the people around the intended victim so that you become commonplace, a fact of life like an armchair or a side table. Then no one questioned you when you came close. No one saw as you slipped the stiletto between the ribs, or dropped the poison in the drink.

Or attacked a man in a small neighborhood park.

She looked down at the noble face of the man who lay so quietly, his black hair spread on the pillow. He did not look peaceful. He looked worn and deeply ill, his closed eyes bruised with dark shadows. The coverlet had been pulled up to his bare shoulders. Sometimes when the injuries were so severe, a physician simply had to stop healing because an abused body could only take so much Power coursing through it. This must have been the case with Riordan, for she could see the uneven bump of bandages underneath the covering.

No one was watching, and it was, after all, such a simple thing she needed to do. She reached out a hand and touched his temple, feeling the pulse of life underneath the pads of her fingers. Then, tenderly, she stroked the silken black hair from his forehead. It was the most audacious thing she had ever done, stealing this one moment.

Some extra sense made her turn her head. Niniane stood a few feet away, staring at her. The Queen's gaze was very wide and startled, and far too perceptive. Xanthe snatched her hand back and cleared her throat. Turned away. Turned back again. She was in an agony of embarrassment.

Niniane stopped her by simply putting a hand on her arm.

Meanwhile, Tiago saw the doctors out the door and closed it firmly on everybody else again. He turned back to join Niniane and Xanthe, looking down at Riordan.

"We'll have to investigate everybody," he said. "That includes everyone in his household, of course, and his staff at the palace. The neighbors will need to be canvassed."

"I know who did this," Niniane said through set teeth.

"You think you know who instigated this," Tiago corrected as he slanted a dark look at her. "It could have actually been carried out by almost anybody."

Xanthe said, "We came through the park where his servants found him. It is a small neighborhood space, with a few trees and benches, and a little shrubbery around the edges. There is almost no place to hide. If someone lay in wait for him there, they would have looked out of place. And there would have been the sounds of the attack. No one heard or came to help him, so it is likely the inhabitants of the neighboring houses were out at some function. His attackers probably watched and waited for just such a time."

Tiago and Niniane both regarded her with thoughtful, set expressions. "There were any number of dinners and parties this evening," Niniane said.

"I'll track down who received which invitations, and which ones they attended," Tiago said.

"Sir, your grace, please give me leave to investigate this," Xanthe said between her teeth.

"No," Tiago said. "This hunt is mine." He looked at down Niniane as he rubbed her back. "He cannot remain here while I investigate. We will need to move him to the palace where we can guarantee his safety, at least until I clear his servants."

Niniane remained focused so intently on Xanthe, she had to control the urge to twitch. It was impossible to tell what the Queen was thinking. Would she say anything about Xanthe's inappropriate behavior? Perhaps Niniane might even dismiss her. Xanthe braced herself.

Niniane said to her, "You have a cottage, about an hour's walk outside the city."

Whatever she expected, it hadn't been this. She blinked, and said, "Yes, your grace."

"It is quiet there? Away from major traffic of any kind?" When she nodded, Niniane looked up at Tiago. "What about neighbors?"

He tilted his head, considering her. "I got a good look at the land when I flew out there. There aren't any neighbors in sight of the cottage. The nearest one is a farm some distance away."

"I think we should take Aubrey there," Niniane said. "The cottage is quiet and out of the way. Until you finish investigating his palace staff and his household servants, the cottage would be the safest place for him. Xanthe can tend to him and guard him, and nobody will ever think to look for him there."

Astonishment held Xanthe so frozen she didn't blink, or breathe.

Tiago murmured to Niniane, "There you go again, not following a logical path from A to B then C. You always leap to some part of the alphabet that's a complete surprise to me, and yet it makes perfect sense."

A ghost of a sparkle came into the Queen's exhausted gaze. She asked, "It's a good idea, isn't it?"

"It's an excellent idea. I can take him to the roof, change and fly him there. I'll cloak myself so that nobody will know. He'll just vanish into thin air." He looked at Xanthe. "You will do it, won't you—guard him until we have found those responsible for this?"

Xanthe's hands shook as she turned to stare at Riordan's still face. He would be in her home, where almost no one ever came. He would convalesce in her bed. She could make certain that he was safe.

"Oh, my lord," she whispered. "Yes."

Chapter Four
The Depths

He woke.

Pain and exhaustion pinned him. He lay in a strange bed, in a strange room. The day was unusually quiet. There were no sounds of carriages or distant voices, just the occasional call from birds. Sunshine slanted in through a partially shaded, open window. Wind wafted gently into the room. There was a doorway to another room, where another open doorway showed flagstones and the edge of green grass.

Strange covers were drawn up over his chest and arms. They bore down heavily on him. He tried to move and couldn't, and while he was trying, he fell asleep.

When he woke again, daylight had almost faded completely. It was much cooler and the room was filled with deep shadows. He recognized nothing about the scene except for the pain he was in. His bones ached, a deep insistent throb, and he was still exhausted.

An echo of clashing swords drifted through his memory. Probably someone had kidnapped him. He found it hard to care at the moment, except if he was not dead, the whole event would turn into another long, dreary saga.

He closed his eyes and drifted.

The memory of the swordfight came back, stronger and clearer. The park, late at night. A triad of attackers. He fought hard, and he might have had a chance except for that first crippling blow that struck him from behind.

If he hadn't sensed something and started to turn, the blow would have killed him. As it was, it cut through several major muscles in his back. Still he had tried, putting viciousness into every thrust and parry, while his defeat flowed down over the back of his legs in a hot red tide and he knew he was going to die, and really, in some ways, the realization was a relief.

A quiet noise broke through the memory. Someone moved around in the other room, and his eyes flared open again. Of course he wasn't alone.

A slim straight figure appeared in the doorway then stepped into the room. The waning light fell on the familiar features of the Queen's new attendant, Xanthe Tenanye.

Bitter disappointment lanced through him, and a sickeningly familiar sense of betrayal. He said savagely, "Better me than the Queen, I suppose, or have you taken her too?"

A smile had begun to spread over her face, and something had lightened her gaze. She froze, both smile and light dying. Expressionless and calm, she said with exquisite politeness, "You have been unconscious since the attack last night. I will need to check your bandages soon, my lord, but that can wait until the morning. There is broth and bread. You may not yet feel ready to eat, but it would be good if you could drink some broth. You almost d—you lost a lot of fluid."

Almost died. Yes, that sounded about right.

He fixed his gaze on the ceiling's rafters. Since he was not really suicidal, and he had not died, he supposed he'd better take in some sustenance. He would need strength for the upcoming ordeal. He bit out, "Very well."

She seemed to hesitate. Then out of the corner of his eye, he saw her bow her head and leave the room.

Why had she started to smile? That look in her eyes. She looked like he had kicked her in the teeth before that perfect, polite wall of hers had come down.

Come to think of it, why was he bandaged?

His assailants had not fought to overcome him. They had fought to kill him.

Realization stung him. He said, "Xanthe."

He could not put much strength into his voice, but she heard him anyway and appeared again in the doorway of the bedroom. This time she remained in shadow, and he could not see her face, although he knew what she would look like. Perfect, expressionless.

"I am an old fool who has let himself become ruled by bitterness and disappointment," he said tiredly. His meager strength was waning fast again. "I apologize for the conclusion I leapt to so erroneously. You did not deserve that."

She moved forward quickly, coming into the light, and there was expression back in her face, shimmering in her eyes. "Please do not distress yourself, my lord. You have been badly injured, and you awakened to find yourself in a strange place with no explanation."

He closed his eyes. "Yes."

Gentle fingers touched his forehead then his cheek. Checking for fever, he supposed. Her hand felt warm, so he doubted he had one.

"Where am I?" he whispered. Speaking out loud was too hard to continue.

"You are at my cottage," Xanthe said softly. Her quiet, calm demeanor was soothing. "Her grace and Tiago decided you should be brought completely outside of Adriyel, while they searched for who did this to you. Tiago brought you here in secret. Except for the Queen, Tiago and I, no one knows where you are. You are safe."

He should never have doubted this straight, shining woman's dedication. The damn covers still felt as heavy as a ton of bricks, prohibiting gesture. He felt the urge to turn his face to her warm, gentle hand, and a scant moment later, he was shocked to realize he had. "Thank you."

She cupped his cheek. "I am so—glad that I could somehow be of service to you."

"What do we know?" Inevitably his thoughts turned to the Ealduns. Had they discovered that Sebrin was digging into the case they had built against him? They wouldn't have been goaded to violence by the threat of any of that becoming known, would they? After all, it would have come to light anyway had the lawsuit been allowed to continue.

He hadn't heard from the junior secretary since the other man had left Adriyel for the Ealduns' family holdings, but then he hadn't expected to, as it was a journey of some days away. Was Sebrin all right?

Xanthe did not bother to ask him what he meant. She said, "Nothing yet. We transported you as soon as the physicians had finished working on you. Tiago will return in a few days with more supplies. We can hope to learn something then. I'll fetch the broth and bread."

"Do not trouble yourself," he mumbled around the cotton that seemed to have filled his mouth. "I'm afraid it will have to wait until morning."

"Then rest well, my lord."

She sounded far away. Any further thought or speculation disappeared into cool evening shadow.

Over the next three days, he slept, and woke, and slept again, until he could not tell if his body ached from the healing wounds or from being confined so long to bed. When he was awake, he lay watching the line of sunlight from the nearby window move along the corner of the quilt, his mind a tired blank. If he made any noise at all, and quite often even when he didn't, Xanthe was there, patiently spooning broth or water between his lips. She changed his bandages a few times, and it was such an utter misery he had to bite his lip to keep from moaning.

On the morning of the fourth day, birdsong woke him early. He moved unguardedly and swore. Suddenly

Xanthe was leaning over him, her dark gaze concerned. "It's all right," he said. "I just forgot." His mouth and throat were a burning desert. "I need a drink, please."

"Of course. I have some water here." She turned away and back to him, holding a cup. "I'm going to lift up your head up."

They had established a routine. He nodded. She slid an arm under his shoulders, bracing him as she lifted gently and held the cup to his mouth. He drank slowly, savoring the cool liquid sliding down his throat. She cradled him against her breast. When he had finished drinking all that he wanted, he leaned his head against her, savoring the warm contact with her body even more than he had the liquid.

If artifice had a scent, to him it smelled like Naida's perfumes. He had thrown out everything in her bedroom and had it scrubbed from ceiling to floor, yet now and then he still swore that he caught a whiff of her musky perfume. It made him nauseous.

Xanthe smelled nothing of artifice. She had a clean, simple scent, like sunshine and soap.

She asked, "Any more?"

He felt the small vibration of her voice against his temple and cheek. Reluctantly, he said, "No, thank you."

She eased him back onto his pillows. She looked serious, intent. "I should check your bandages again."

"Certainly," he said, bracing himself.

He had to give her credit. She made the unpleasant task as painless as possible. Her perfect expressionless face was back, insisting there was an invisible wall between them as her gentle hands unwound bandages and she checked the wounds.

He looked down at his bare body dispassionately as she worked. He had no embarrassment over his nudity, and he supposed he was made well enough, but the long gashes were red and ugly, and the wound to his back ached and throbbed insistently. He would have to take care not to tear open the knitting muscle.

"This is good," she murmured. "I think we can leave them off now."

"Hoopla," he said. He gave her a one-sided smile. "I actually mean that."

She grinned. "Do you want some more broth?"

"Gods, no," he said, and she laughed. He told her with surprise, "I'm really hungry."

"Excellent. I found some quails eggs yesterday evening. I will bring you some breakfast in a little bit."

She gathered up the bandages and left the room, returning shortly with scrambled eggs and pan biscuits that had been toasted to a golden brown. She settled into a sitting position on the bed beside him. "My apologies for the simple fare. Tiago will be coming some time day, which is a good thing, since our food supply has dwindled. We've got tea, oil and dry oats. If he's detained for any reason, I will have to do a bit of foraging and hunting."

"This is wonderful," he said in all truthfulness. The steaming eggs were golden and the pan biscuits were delicious. He ate all of the eggs and a biscuit, and then with the abruptness of a convalescent tumbled headlong into sleep.

The sound of voices woke him. Tiago and Niniane were talking with Xanthe in the next room. "This is a wonderful place," Niniane said.

"It is very small," Xanthe said. "My father built it for us after my mother died."

"Your father was a true craftsman. It's beautifully done. The furniture is lovely, and so is the floor."

Aubrey glanced over the edge of the bed at the planed hardwood floors that bore the smooth patina of age. "We brought half the marketplace with us," Tiago said.

"And this bag is full of books," said Niniane. "This one is full of clothes for Aubrey. And this one is full of games. You have plenty here with which to occupy yourselves, as soon as Aubrey is feeling up to it."

"We certainly do," said Xanthe. "This is all so much more than I expected."

Niniane said, "We wanted to make sure you had everything you needed, in case we were unable to return right away."

Xanthe asked quickly, "There are problems?"

"There are complications," Tiago said, stressing the last word. "None of it is anything we can't handle, but we are busy. And Niniane and I have both agreed that no one else is to know that Aubrey is here. You will be on your own until we can return again."

"Yes, sir."

Aubrey clenched his fists and contemplated getting out of bed. He felt immensely better than he had even earlier that morning, and he could tell that he had turned a corner. He eased himself to a sitting position awkwardly. Any unwary movement made his back flare with fiery pain. Breathing deeply, he eased his legs over the edge of the bed.

"How is Aubrey?" Niniane asked.

Aubrey said hoarsely, "I'm awake."

He listened to a symphony of footsteps, one quick, light patter, another light step with a longer stride, and a deeper, heavier tread. He checked to make sure that the sheet was wrapped around his hips as Niniane burst into the bedroom. She threw herself at him, pulling up just before she made contact to put her arms carefully around him.

"I cannot tell you how scared I was for you," she whispered.

He hugged her as he looked over her head at Tiago and at Xanthe. He said gently, "The scare is all over with now." He met Tiago's black gaze. "What has happened since the attack?"

"We are not here to discuss details of the investigation," Tiago said. "Your assailants will not get away unpunished. That's all you need to know, until we come back for you and tell you that you can return home."

Aubrey's face hardened. He opened his mouth to argue, and Niniane put a hand to his cheek, turning him to look at her. Her face was sober, eyes still moist. "Aubrey, you nearly died."

"I know that," he snapped.

"Then listen to me, because I am very serious and I mean every word," Niniane told him. "Your job is to get better. Rest, eat good food, soak up sunshine and heal. That's all. You cannot work. You will not leave this place. This is your safe haven for now. Tiago will return with more food in a week. In the meantime, we will not stop until we have in custody everyone who is responsible for what happened to you. You will be able to come home soon enough, and then you'll have your answers."

He gritted his teeth as rage coursed through him. Not rage at Niniane, but at the people who had attacked him. It was hard to let go of it. After a moment he said, "I will stay until I am completely healed. Then I can ensure my own safety."

"No, Aubrey." The Queen's gaze was adamant. "I am ordering you to stay until I say that you can leave."

"Niniane," he said.

"Oh, I know you're mad at me now. Deal with it." She hugged him again.

He set his teeth but put an arm around her. Looking at Tiago, he said, "At least do one thing for me. I want you to check on one of my staff. His name is Sebrin. I sent him to uncover what he could about the Ealduns' lawsuit, and I hadn't heard from him since."

Tiago and Niniane shared a long, inscrutable look before Tiago promised, "I'll look into it."

Niniane stood. "I'm sorry our visit is so short, but we can't stay any longer." She looked at Xanthe. "Take care of him."

"I will," Xanthe promised.

She trailed behind Niniane and Tiago who left. Aubrey breathed evenly as he glared at the open window. He listened to their voices fade as they moved away from the cottage. If he thought he could stand without falling, he would have followed them to argue.

After a few minutes Xanthe returned. She moved around in the other room then appeared in his doorway carrying two large canvas bags on her shoulders. He glowered at her, which was a totally useless display of petulance as she did not look at him directly. She wore her perfect expressionless face again.

He had been amused by that smooth façade of hers before, but now it was beginning to grate on him. Silence reigned in the room as she opened first one bag and pulled out a pile of folded clothes and boots. She set them on the bed beside him then opened the other bag and pulled out twenty books. Some of them were American paperbacks, and a few were Dark Fae. He glanced at the titles as she stacked them neatly on the small, simple bedside table. None of the books were nonfiction.

Xanthe returned to the pile of clothes on the bed and broke the silence. "Would you like a pair of trousers and a shirt?"

His hand shot out to circle her wrist. She stilled and looked down at his hand. "As soon as I am better, you will take me back to Adriyel."

Her dark gaze lifted to meet his. "No, my lord."

He said, his voice edged, "I did not ask you. I ordered you to."

One of her silken eyebrows raised, a small quirk of reaction. "You may issue as many orders as you like, but I am not obligated to obey you," she said. "I am not your servant. I am the Queen's. You may be willing to defy her orders, but I will not disrespect or disobey her."

There was that loyalty of hers, straight and unwavering. He thought back to his disappointed sense of betrayal when he had so briefly thought she had kidnapped him, and his unruly temper subsided.

He remarked in a much milder tone, "I'm acting like an ass, aren't I?"

Her demeanor softened. "You're angry, and understandably so. It's hard to have your movements restricted, especially when you feel the need to act."

"This has happened to you too," he said. "You must stay here with me."

One corner of her mouth lifted. "Truly, it is not a hardship. I want to do it. But before her grace came up with this idea, I had asked to be the one to hunt for your attackers. Tiago denied me, and it was very hard. He's hunting for all those responsible, himself."

She had wanted to hunt down those who attacked him? He blinked, and his grip loosened.

The last several days had given him a deep, visceral knowledge of her, the timbre of her voice, her scent, the gentle touch of her hands on his body. Following an impulse to learn more about her by touch, he let his fingers slide over her forearm as he slowly let go of her. The texture of her skin was silken, warm.

She took in a quick, near silent breath. As he stared into her eyes he saw her pupils dilate.

She reacted to his touch.

What was he doing? He frowned and released her fully.

She angled her face away as she gathered up the pile of clothes. "Please leave trousers and a shirt," he said.

She nodded and did so, then took the rest of the clothes to set them on the nearby dresser. Afterward, she turned to him, not quite looking at him. "Do you require assistance with dressing?"

He hesitated as he struggled with his pride. It wasn't just his rage; all his emotions were unruly. Normally even tempered, he felt like a stranger to himself. At last, he admitted, "I don't know."

She glanced at his face quickly and nodded. "Call if you have need."

"Thank you."

She stepped out of the room, and he shook out the trousers. Those he could manage, one leg at a time, although his muscles shook when he stood upright to pull them over his hips. The shirt was something else entirely. He could slide one arm into a sleeve, but could not flex his back muscles enough to fully don it.

Instead of calling out to her, he stood again, forcing his knees to lock and accept his full weight. Then he walked carefully across the room, his bare feet making no sound on the smooth floorboards. When he reached the doorway, he leaned one shoulder against its support and looked curiously around the other room.

It was more spacious than the bedroom, with a large kitchen cupboard and shelves along one wall, a table and two chairs, and two more armchairs positioned in front of the fireplace. There was a sideboard with a basin and bucket for washing dishes and preparing meals. A sheathed sword in a shoulder harness hung on a simple hook beside the doorway that stood open to the sunny morning.

All of the furniture was made of plain, solid oak that had been polished to a warm golden color. The armchairs had seat cushions that looked worn and comfortable. As with many Dark Fae country cottages, the large fireplace was the heart of the house, a true cooking fireplace with walk-in room and a swiveling iron bar from which hung a cooking pot.

Beside the fireplace was a shadowed alcove with a curtain pushed open. He could see the edge of a copper tub. There was also a simple pallet on the floor. He paused at that thoughtfully, looking back into 'his' room. There was only one bed in the cottage, and he was using it.

Xanthe was busy unpacking two more large canvas bags. She looked at each package, container or jar interestedly, muttering to herself as she set the items on the table, which was already piled high with fresh fruits and vegetables.

He opened his mouth to ask for her help but then hesitated. Instead, obeying again some nameless impulse, he tilted his head and watched her work. She had a quiet, peaceful demeanor, and she looked comfortable, at home with her own company. For the first time, he realized that she wasn't dressed in a palace black uniform, but instead wore a soft looking, somewhat worn tunic and trousers. Her hair was braided, but not as tightly as usual, and the dark length shone with auburn highlights in the slice of sunlight that fell across her back and shoulders.

His gaze lingered on the gentle curve of her cheek then dropped to the swell of her breasts, where he had rested his head earlier. Her hips were slight and trim but definitely feminine. She was not as tall as he, but her legs were lean and long.

She looked up toward the doorway, saw that he was watching her, and a delicate tinge of color washed over her face. She glanced at his shirt that hung off one shoulder and set aside a wax wheel of cheese to walk over to him quickly.

"You should have said something," she said.

He raised his eyebrows. "Did you just scold me?"

She jerked to a halt, the color in her cheeks deepening. "I—I'm sorry, my lord."

She looked so flustered, he found himself smiling. He asked gently, "Xanthe, would you mind helping me slip into this blasted shirt?"

Her gaze flew up to his, to his bare shoulders and chest, and darted away. "Not at all," she said. She sounded winded.

He could barely stand on his feet, and his body still throbbed with pain. But something else stirred, something that had been buried under grief and anger and had lain dormant for a long while.

She came closer to carefully ease him fully into the shirt, and his back muscles protested only a small bit as she supported the full weight of his arm.

He was taller than she was by half a head. He bent his head close to hers, inhaling her fresh, clean scent. "Thank you."

She tilted her head slightly, so that they stood almost cheek to cheek. If she raised her head a little more, if he lowered his….

"You're welcome," she whispered.

This was too intimate. He straightened. "I see Tiago was not joking when he said they brought half the marketplace."

She widened her gaze. "There are even biscuits and a pot of clotted cream. I haven't reached the bottom of the bags yet. If I fish for supper occasionally and forage for sun potatoes and fresh greens, we have enough food for weeks." She paused then asked hesitantly, "Would you like to sit at the table while I put things away?"

For a moment he was tempted but another wave of dizziness washed over him. He gritted his teeth, hating his own weakness. "Perhaps later," he said. "Right now, I think I need to lie down again."

"Of course." She stepped close, put her arm around his waist and helped him back to the bed.

Darkness danced around the edge of his vision. He muttered, "I've taken your only bed and put you on the floor."

"That does not matter."

He eased back onto the pillows. "It matters to me."

The darkness grew closer, hazing his mind. As if from a great distance, he felt her tuck the sheet over him. He thought he heard her say, "That is why people care about you so much."

Then his unruly emotions and wayward mind grew quiet, as the darkness took him over completely.

Chapter Five
The Dance

Xanthe took the perishables like the eggs and clotted cream, loaded them carefully into the wire well basket, and then lowered them into the cool deep water of the well. She kept a few of the eggs out to boil them. While those cooked, she found storage places for rest of the food.

There were also biscuits, fresh bread, jams and jellies, cheese, both fresh and salted meat, nuts, three kinds of tea, butter, flour, barley, sugar, fruits and vegetables. Sweet potatoes. There were even three bars of soap that smelled like honeyed almonds and were rich enough that fine ladies would not distain using them. This cottage had never seen such rich fare.

Xanthe was no fancy cook, but she could prepare good, plain meals, and all the luxuries from the market would help to dress up anything she might offer. By the time Aubrey awakened again, she had a substantial lunch prepared of the last of the chicken, sautéed turnip greens, boiled eggs, and bread, butter and jam. In small bowls were fresh berries sprinkled with sugar.

She was just about to retrieve the clotted cream from the well when she heard his quiet footsteps. She turned as he entered the room. He ran his hands through loose raven hair. His clothes were rumpled, and his feet were still bare. It was shocking to see him in any way less than meticulously groomed and in formal clothing. As she studied his stance and angular features, she was pleased to see that he was much steadier already.

He said, "I see that you have been busy."

"Are you hungry?"

His gaze lit upon the contents on the table. "I am."

She had not been sure how to lay out the meal, if he might need to stay in bed or if he would rather she did not eat with him. But this was, after all, her home. There was only one place to sit and eat, and also, he had not seemed to mind in the slightest when she had joined him and Tiago for breakfast, so she had laid two settings.

His gait was steady, if a bit stiff, as he walked over to ease into one of the chairs. The reality of sitting across from him and eating alone with him started to sink in.

She remembered the clotted cream and said awkwardly, "I almost forgot something—I'll be right back."

He snagged hold of her hand when she would have walked away. Her insides churned at the warm grasp. Although she would have given anything for him not to have been so badly wounded, already there were so many moments of this experience that she would hold close and treasure afterward. Chief among them was every time he touched her.

He looked up at her. The gold of the sun glimmered in his light gray eyes. "Thank you for this, Xanthe. Thank you for everything."

She turned her hand to clasp his and press briefly at his lean fingers, as she said, entirely truthfully, "It is truly my pleasure, my lord."

"I expect you to start calling me Aubrey," he said as he returned the squeeze of her fingers and released her. "After all, as you so eloquently pointed out, you are not my servant."

He was nobility, while she was a commoner. She forced her lips to move. "That would not be appropriate."

He winked at her. "As Tiago would say, screw appropriate."

Winked. At her.

She should probably respond in some manner to what he had said, but her mind seized up, so she gave up and fled the cottage.

When she drew up the wire basket from the well to retrieve the pot of cream, she splashed cold water on her face and stood for a moment with her head bent, the water dripping from her nose and chin.

"Aubrey," she whispered. The sweet pain, that honey-eyed stiletto, pierced her all over again.

When she returned indoors, he was watching the dying flames in the cookfire, his food untouched. He had waited for her. That embarrassed her for some reason. She opened the pot and set it on the table as she slipped into her seat. She muttered, "For the berries."

Aubrey picked up his knife and fork. "Niniane knows I have a sweet tooth. It was kind of her to indulge it."

"We have steak for this evening," she told him. "And a roast for tomorrow. After that, it will be fish and salt meat. If you like, I can use the roast for a field stew." A field stew was traditional hunter's fare and often combined sweet and savory flavors.

"I love field stew. It's the only thing I know how to cook, although it has been some time since I have actually hunted." He gave her another smile to add to her treasure of memories. "Niniane was right, this cottage is charming. Your father did a wonderful job."

"Thank you." She looked around as if seeing it through fresh eyes. To someone of Aubrey's stature and wealth, it must seem like a very humble place.

"Where is your father now?"

The bite she had taken turned to dust in her mouth. She forced herself to swallow. "He was one of the palace guards who died the night Urien seized power."

Aubrey paused eating as well. "I'm very sorry."

"It was a long time ago." She gave him a quick smile. "I was only a new recruit in the army, so I was nowhere near the palace that night."

He studied her. "You stayed a soldier despite what had happened?"

Her shoulders stiffened. "I did. I worked hard and eventually became a palace guard. I had a dream of one day taking Urien completely by surprise and sinking my knife into his back. The chance never came. When Tiago employed me, I told that to him in the interview. He liked that I could be so patient while I looked for an opportunity. He called the last two hundred years my hunting season." She lifted her gaze to Aubrey's face. Would he be repulsed by what she had just confessed?

He didn't look in the least repulsed. His expression was open and accepting. As they finished the main portion of their meal, he took the pot of cream, spooning some onto her berries first before he helped himself. The small courtesy warmed her.

He said, "After Urien killed Rhian and Shaylee who were my friends, the hardest thing I ever did was to remain Chancellor when he renewed my appointment. In fact, several of my other friends could not accept it and they cut me off. A few have begun speaking to me again, but I no longer care for their regard."

She said, "You hated Urien too."

"Of course I did," he said. His face had turned hard, the angles of the graceful bones standing out against his pale skin. "Passionately. It kept me awake at night. It poisoned the savor of my meals. But the Dark Fae and the welfare of Adriyel meant more to me than my own rancor. I tempered Urien's actions whenever I possibly could, went behind his back when I thought I could get away with it, and did everything in my power to help steer the congress and the courts on a steady path."

Xanthe set aside her spoon. She said carefully, "I respect Niniane as my Queen, and in a very short time, I have grown to love her, so please do not mistake what I say. What you did has not gone unrecognized. I, along with everybody that I know, hoped that you would be crowned king. Those so-called friends of yours—while their first reaction was understandable, to go all that time without speaking to you was exceedingly short sighted, judgmental and cruel."

The hardness eased gradually from his face as he listened. He gave her a faint smile that was little more than a crinkling of his eyes at the edges. "Thank you." He scraped the bottom of his bowl. "This was a delicious meal, and the company was even more delightful. I absolutely refuse to fall asleep again."

She laughed. "Sleep is your body's way of recovering, but if you would rather, we can spread a blanket for you under a tree while you explore the pile of books Niniane and Tiago left."

"That sounds perfect." He watched while she cleared the table and stacked the dishes in the basin. Then he held his side with a wince as he yawned widely.

She suspected his fight against sleep would not last long. Not only had his injuries taxed his resources, so had the healing. The physician had ordered at least two sevendays of convalescence for a reason.

She took a blanket outside for him and shook it out in the shade of a large elm tree that was located near the front door. He appeared a few moments later, carrying three books, and struggled to kneel on the blanket. She hovered beside him, anxious to help, but his savage expression held her back.

When he was seated on the ground, he eased himself back until he was prone. She went into the cottage and returned with a pillow.

"Thank you," he said. The skin around his mouth was white.

"You're welcome." She watched for a moment as he selected one of the books and began to read. Then she went to draw water to clean the dishes.

When she was finished, she looked outside. His eyes were closed, his book resting on his chest. She grinned. Each time he fell asleep he woke up stronger. This time, he might even wake up grumpier.

After she had washed and put away the dishes, she puttered around for a bit. She made the bed and boiled the bandages that he had worn. When they were thoroughly cleansed, she hung them in the sun. After they dried, she would roll and store them.

The rest of the cottage was already tidy. There was more than enough food. In a few days, she would have to do laundry, but for now there wasn't anything that required attention until it was time to cook supper.

An invisible leash pulled her to the sleeping man underneath the shade tree. Silently she eased herself down to sit on one corner of the blanket. She felt as guilty as if she were stealing, but she couldn't help herself. Studying him at leisure without fear of discovery was an almost unimaginable luxury.

He did not look quite so desperately ill, but he still looked worn. Shadows under his eyes lingered, as did the brackets of pain around his mouth. Tenderness pulled at her.

It was one thing to admire him from a distance for all the fine things he embodied. It was totally different to grow to know him a little, and to see the real man behind the reputation. He struggled with his temper, chafed at illness and injury, carried shadows of loneliness in those kind eyes.

Instead of showing her that her idol had feet of clay, all these things served to highlight just how outstanding his long service to his country had been. How many times had he felt endangered by Urien? Probably too often to count. When he had lain awake at night, did he, too, wonder if he might die friendless and alone?

If he had cared at all about his wife—and she believed that he had for he was a caring man—he had no doubt relied upon her companionship and drew comfort from her support, which would have made the crimes that she had committed doubly terrible for him.

She watched him quietly as the sun traveled through the sky and the dappled shade moved across his long, relaxed body. When he began to stir, she shot to her feet and fled into the house. She had her weapons laid out on the table and her sword drawn and was busy polishing and sharpening blades when Aubrey's shadow fell into the room. She kept her head tucked down, gaze focused on her task.

He said nothing as he stood and watched her. The moment spun on an enchanted spindle until it drew out, long and golden like a thread of dyed flax pulling taut between them. She would not look up. She could not. She did not feel in control of herself, and she was terrified at what might show in her eyes.

Finally he moved quietly into the bedroom.

Her fingers shook. She nicked one on the blade she had just sharpened. She sucked the injured finger and thought, I am a fool.

When she finished with her task, she sheathed all her weapons and hung them in their customary spot beside the cottage door. Somehow the day had fled so that it was time to cook supper. She had set sweet potatoes to bake in the coals of the lunch cook fire, so all that she needed to do was grill the steaks and prepare a fresh salad of mixed greens and vegetables.

She stepped outside to collect an armful of wood. When she came back into the cottage, Aubrey appeared. He was still barefoot, and he had unbuttoned his shirt. It hung open on his wide shoulders. The wounds on his long, lean torso were already fading. This time when Aubrey raised his hands to his loose hair, he worked with a wince to tie the length back with a leather strip. It caused his chest muscles to bunch and flow under his skin.

She looked at the rippling hollows of his flat abdomen where his muscles were tightened, and her breath grew restricted. She had to force enough air into lungs to tell him, "Once the fire is ready, supper won't be long."

He wore a tense, sour expression. "I dislike watching you fix meals and fuss."

She stared down at the wood she carried, blinking. "Have I fussed? I am sorry. But we must eat."

He moved abruptly. "That is not what I meant. I'm the one who is sorry. You have not fussed. You've done nothing but show me patience and kindness, even when I'm sure I've been tactless and did not deserve it. I am frustrated that you are doing all the work. I dislike watching you labor while I do nothing." He gave a sharp sigh. "I am unused to doing nothing."

That she could understand. She was unused to doing nothing as well. She looked at him sideways and gave him a sly smile. "It sounds as though you are beginning to feel better."

He chuckled. "I must be, since my temper has turned so foul. What can I do to help?"

Shocked, her gaze flew wide. "Nothing!"

He advanced on her with a determined expression, and she backed up until her shoulders hit the wall behind her. "I do not accept that answer."

"You are the one who was severely injured. I am perfectly healthy, and it is my job to look after you and do the work." She hugged the armful of wood as he tried to take the top few logs. "Stop that! You're still healing, and you might strain one of those wounds."

"I am well aware of what my body can and cannot do, thank you." He tugged and she pulled back, until he pointed out in a plaintive voice, "You know this tug of war can't be good for me."

She stared at him in wounded astonishment. Oh, that was playing entirely naughty. She stopped instantly, her hold loosening. As he took the top logs from her armload, she glared at him, mouth folded tight in disapproval.

He paused, and one corner of his mouth tilted up as he studied her. "You should see what you look like right now," he told her.

"I have no idea what you're talking about," she muttered as she hitched her remaining armload up higher.

He folded his mouth tight and glared at her.

Completely off kilter, she stared, and her own mouth dropped open. "I don't look that bad!"

"No," he agreed, the expression vanishing. "You are much prettier than me."

"Don't be ridiculous!" She scuttled sideways to get around him then rushed to the fireplace to throw her armload onto the hearth. It scattered wood debris everywhere, and the floor would have to be swept again. She didn't care. Then her next thought just fell out of her mouth. "You're the most handsome man I know."

The instant the words left her lips, she would have snatched them out of the air if she could. Her face burned.

He moved up beside her and squatted to ease the logs he had purloined onto the hearth with hers.

She watched with round, unblinking eyes as he straightened and turned to face her.

He thinks I'm pretty?

He was smiling, and it looked satisfied and very male. "So you think I'm handsome."

She scrambled to backtrack somehow. Heaven only knew where her poise had gone. The afternoon sun must have baked it out of her head. "Of course you look—distinguished," she accused. "You know perfectly well you do."

Of all the ridiculous things to say. She was going from bad to worse. She spun on her heel, retreated to put the table between them and began pulling food items off the shelves without really looking at what she was doing.

He followed at a leisurely pace across the room, almost as if he was stalking her.

Then he came all the way around the table.

He—what was he doing?

"You didn't say distinguished before," he pointed out. "You said handsome. I remember that fact quite fondly."

"DidIIhadn'tnoticed," she mumbled all in a rush. She had forgotten what she was supposed to be doing. If she had ever known in the first place.

"Xanthe, are you shy?" he murmured. "I didn't know assassins could be shy. This realization is remarkable."

"Don't be stupid, I'm never shy," she blurted. She had disrobed in front of dozens of other soldiers countless of times. She'd had sex with no more privacy than what the cover of a blanket might offer, and she had probably heard every crude joke or epithet the army had in its repertoire. "And I'm not an assassin any longer, I'm a guard."

"Semantics, my dear." His lean, angular features were lit with delight. All shadows and marks of pain had vanished. He looked like an entirely different man from the ill, unconscious man that Tiago had brought into her cottage. He glanced over all the items she had placed at random on the table. His sleek eyebrows rose. "So we are having honey, cheese, onions and tea for supper?"

"Of course not!" Her cheeks grew hotter. She scrambled for some kind excuse for her erratic behavior. "I was just going to dust off the shelves."

He picked up the jar of honey. "Were you going to do that before or after you cook?"

She threw up her hands. "You are distracting me from what I'm supposed to be doing!"

He was laughing then, his face creased with open enjoyment, eyes dancing. "Is that what I'm doing, distracting you? I thought I was teasing you."

Witnessing him in this unpredictable, playful mode was definitely much more composure-destroying than when he had winked at her. She rushed at him and snatched the jar out of his hands. "Get out of my kitchen, so I can have some hope of cooking something edible."

He pointed out, "Your kitchen is half the cottage."

She ducked her head. "You could go outside."

"I've been outside for a significant part of the day already."

"Go to bed then."

"I have spent a significant part of the day there too," he said softly. "And I feel extraordinarily guilty every time I lie in that soft bed. Inevitably I end up thinking of you, and this hard pallet on the floor that must be so very uncomfortable."

Her breathing hitched again. She picked up the cheese and turned away to start setting things back on the shelves. "I keep telling you, I don't mind in the slightest. Believe me, I have bunked down under much worse conditions many times."

"That doesn't make me feel better." He handed her the onions to set back in their place, and as she turned around again, he handed her the tin of tea. "I propose that I begin to help with the chores around here." When she opened her mouth to argue, he forestalled her. "I will only do what I feel capable of doing, and each day I will increase my activity. That will help me regain my strength much faster. I simply cannot laze my days away and watch as you shoulder the burden for doing everything. I don't have it in me."

She sighed. Increasing his activity each day would help him heal. She also knew some stretching exercises that he could do to help keep his body limber. He was going to carry scars, and those would stiffen if he wasn't careful. "That makes sense."

"And as soon as my back muscles have healed enough," he said, "you and I are going to start taking turns on that pallet."

"No, we're not," she told him.

"Yes," he said implacably. "We are."

"I won't budge on this," she warned.

His mouth quirked. "What a coincidence; neither will I."

If they grew stubborn about this, they might both end up sleeping on floor pallets. She clapped a hand over her nose and mouth as a snort of laughter escaped her.

If anyone had told her a sevenday ago that she would be arguing with a barefoot Chancellor of the Dark Fae, she would have thought them deranged. Shaking her head, she turned away from him again to set the tea tin on the shelf.

Then she sensed rather than heard him move up close behind her. She stood frozen, the skin at the back of her neck tingling as she felt the heat of his body along her back and thighs. He was very close, perhaps a scant finger's breadth away. She turned her head slightly, her attention consumed by his nearness.

She could see him, just barely, out of the corner of her eye, standing there like the shadow of her most secret dream. He tilted his head and put his lips near her ear, still not coming in physical contact with her anywhere.

He whispered, "Am I really the most handsome man you know?"

His warm breath caressed the thin, sensitive area just behind her jaw. She folded her arms around her middle, shaking. A daring stranger took over her voice. She closed her eyes and heard herself whisper back, "Do you really think I'm pretty?"

Pretty. It was a word used for Dark Fae ladies, with their fine clothes, long pale, soft hands and large, lustrous eyes. It didn't belong to her. Her hands were callused, her skin lightly speckled by the sun. Her feet were callused too. She could kill a man with a single, well placed kick of her bare foot.

The slightest touch stroked along her hair, following the line from her temple, back to her braid. Was that his finger? The end of his nose? It was so light she could almost have believed that she imagined it, yet it sent an intense shiver rippling over her skin. It was—almost as though he nuzzled her. The thought took all the strength out of her knees.

At the nape of her neck, he breathed, "I think you grow more beautiful each time I lay my eyes on you. It's happened every time I woke up to find you there, helping me in some way. All I want to do is look at you, to experience it again."

The moist warm heat of the words felt like a brand. The shiver settled low in her abdomen, and a liquid heat bloomed between her legs. Surely he would not notice if her hand trailed stealthily down her torso to press at the sharp, empty ache.

"Don't play with me just because you're bored." The words were meant to wedge some kind of distance between them and allow sanity back into the room, to cool the insane heat that built so that she could not focus for wanting to tear off all her clothes. Instead they sounded pleading.

"I would never dream of treating you in such a self-indulgent and cavalier manner." He stroked her back, another feather light touch that explored the contour of her shoulder blade and the indentation just underneath where her ribs curved to her spine. "Xanthe, I have not heard you say my name yet."

The same pleading she had heard in her own voice was in his too.

Her regard mattered to him.

Her knees weakened further, and her lips trembled.

She whispered, "Aubrey."

He was silent. She could hear him breathing. Then another brush of sensation at the back of her neck—those were his lips. He had kissed her.

"Thank you, my dear," he whispered in return as he pulled away.

Chapter Six

Sacrifice

Aubrey backed from Xanthe, his emotions more unruly than ever. Arousal coursed through his body, more powerful than the lingering aches and pains. He had grown hard, and his swollen cock, surprised into life after a year of dullness and disinterest, demanded attention most urgently.

The sensation of her soft, warm skin lingered on his lips. He licked them.

He wanted to lick her so much more.

Restlessness, irritation, his growing awareness of her as an attractive female, it had turned into an all too potent cocktail. Teasing her had been impulse. Pursuing as she retreated had been instinct. He had not thought through any of it; it had just happened, and that was unlike him as he was usually thoughtful and deliberate about everything.

His intellect wrestled with his bucking instincts. It was a tough tussle, but intellect—just barely—won.

He turned away and muttered hoarsely, "I'll start helping by laying a fire."

"That would be nice."

Her voice shook, a telltale, vulnerable sound from such a strong, bright woman. The impulse to sexual aggression flared hot and insistent. His instincts weren't going down without a fight.

At the hearth, he forced himself to go down on one knee, and he poked at the ashes of the previous fire to see if any live embers remained. He disturbed a few charred sweet potatoes, and he rolled those over to the side then quickly laid the wood. A few glowing coals remained, and soon the fire was blazing.

He straightened from his crouch and moved to a nearby armchair to tend the fire unnecessarily. The soft sounds of movement behind him seemed as loud as a shout, proclaiming that her presence was close and vital.

He glanced over his shoulder and almost laughed. The crazy woman had put more things on the table again. This time, though, he could see that it all had a theme, fruits and vegetables, so no doubt she had meant to do it. She was chopping greens.

Her face was calm, smooth, perfectly expressionless.

Reaction roared through him. He shook with the urge to stalk over, take the knife from her hand, press her up against the wall and cover her lips with his. Spear into her mouth. Anything to strip away that façade and see what really lay underneath.

Her breathing had been unsteady. She had asked him not to toy with her. Her voice had trembled when she had whispered his name.

She had not been indifferent, gods damn it.

He rubbed his face. Maybe he really had died in the attack, and a demon of lunacy had taken over his body. This kind of impetuosity was completely outside of his normal behavior and deeply unsettling.

His wretched cock still wouldn't bend to his rule either. The air in the cottage had turned much too close and stifling. He rose to his feet and walked out.

Outside, the early evening air was much cooler. After a moment's searching, he found the covered well and drew a bucket of ice cold water.

First he drank thirstily. Then he dumped the rest of it over his head, gasping and shuddering as it cascaded all over his body. *Holy shit.* The sensation was keen as a knife, and just as painful, and a fitting way to force him to contemplate the magnitude of his own folly.

He leaned his palms on the rim of the well as water dripped off of him.

The thing of it was, he couldn't remember a time before when he was ever this attracted to a woman. No doubt it had happened; he had lived a very long time, after all.

But that would have been a younger self in another time. A less tried, greener self.

It wasn't here and now, where he embodied the totality of all of his experiences.

When the beauty of the spirit had come to mean so much more to him than the beauty of the body.

Where he knew a multitude of sorrows and reasons to be wary, and yet he still felt this slow burning, excruciating build-up of need.

Naida had caused him a vicious hurt precisely because he had loved her, but he had never felt anything for her that was remotely like what he was coming to feel for Xanthe. He and Naida had gone through a considered courtship, discussed together the advantages of a partnership together and had come to a mutual agreement. Everything had been very much in character, laid out, predictable.

At the time he thought it had been so very civilized, their relationship solidly grounded in friendship. Really, nothing could compare to the shock of a civilized man who came face to face with his own barbarity.

The smell of cooking steak wafted out of the cottage, and his stomach growled. His appetite for food had come back with a vengeance. It was a solid metaphor, as his appetite for other things had now resurfaced. He had sustained two serious injuries, one spiritual and the other physical, and it appeared that he would end up surviving them both after all.

As for the quiet, reserved Xanthe—he could see nothing to hold him back from going after what he now acknowledged that he wanted. He no longer had any ties or previous commitments. He was free to act on whatever he desired.

Now it was time for his own hunting season.

When she saw him step into the cottage carrying the water bucket, she rushed at him from the hearth, scolding. "You should not be carrying something that heavy so soon!"

He smiled and tilted the bucket slightly to show her the contents. "You are such a ferocious mother hen. It's only half full. I said I would help and I mean to do it. I'll draw all the water for the supper dishes. It will take me twice as long, but that is quite all right as there are no urgent appointments this evening."

After glancing into the bucket, she looked up at him somewhat shamefaced. "I just don't want you to hurt yourself any further."

"I appreciate that," he said, warmed by the evidence of her caring. Deliberately, he leaned forward and pressed his lips to hers, a full, firm, yet brief caress. All too soon, he pulled away. The sensation of her lips, softened in surprise, was branded on his mouth.

She stood absolutely still, her lovely dark eyes very wide.

He would not smile. It might reveal too much triumph. He sidestepped neatly around her and went to the basin to pour water into it. Then he went outside again. By the time he returned, she had hunched over the grilling steaks and she did not look up.

He made three more trips to the well before she set the steaming steaks on the table, and he surveyed the results of his effort with satisfaction. He had drawn plenty of water for the evening dishes. Then he turned to the table. She had created a salad of greens, fresh vegetables, apples and berries, lightly dressed with oil and herbs, to accompany the steaming sweet potatoes and steak.

She also looked exceedingly spooked.

This would have to be a gentle hunt, or his prey might skedaddle.

As he took his seat at the table, he said gravely, "Thank you for another wonderful meal."

Unaccountably, she flushed as she sat as well. "I do not know how to cook the complex delicacies you are no doubt used to eating."

He kept his gaze on the contents of his plate. "Do not confuse what you imagine my lifestyle must be with what you witness at the palace. I much prefer meals like this on a daily basis." He sensed rather than saw her relax a little. They ate in silence. Now that he had turned the corner, he could almost feel the return of health and vigor with every bite of the healthy fare. As he finished, he said, "I would like to take advantage of that bathing alcove this evening, if I might."

She said quickly, "Of course. I'll draw water and put it on to heat while I do the dishes." She glanced up at him and then away, her gaze skittering off like a frightened mouse. "You will carry some scarring from those wounds. It will be good for you to soak in a hot tub with a little oil poured in the water."

He nodded. He would fetch his own bath water if he could, but he had already reached his limit. "If you would be kind enough to draw the water, I will wash the dishes—no, I do not want to hear it, Xanthe." He added that last in a stern, no nonsense voice as she began to speak. "We have already agreed upon this."

She closed her mouth with an audible click of her teeth. After a moment, she muttered, "Agreeing in theory and watching it in practice are two different things."

He said in a very gentle voice, "But you would not deny me anything that is good for me, would you?"

"Of course not," she replied in a strangled whisper, while she looked at him exasperation. He bit back a smile.

By the time he had washed the dishes and put them away, his bath water had heated to a comfortable temperature, and he soaked in the silken, lightly oiled bath until the water had cooled. Then he washed all over, luxuriating in the sensation of cleanliness.

In the pile of clothing Niniane and Tiago had brought for him was a long, warm robe, which he donned afterward. Mercifully his aches were retreating as he healed, but after supper and the light exercise, the bath had done him in.

As he pushed aside the curtain, he saw that Xanthe must have used the basin to wash as well, for her hair was wet and slicked back, and she had donned a soft dark purple shirt and trousers. Full evening had set, and the warmth from the fire mingled pleasantly with the coolness of the air that wafted in from the still open door.

She sat in one of the armchairs, looking at the fire contemplatively, which lit her profile with golden light. Desire glowed deep within him, banked in its own hearth and waiting for the right opportunity to spark into a blaze.

Something had been tickling at his awareness for some time, but he only now paid attention to it. He frowned. "There is something of Power in this room."

"Yes," she said. Her gaze flicked to the mantle. "I will show it to you, if you like."

Did she look guilty? He wondered why.

He walked over to look curiously at the items on the mantel. There was a pipe lying in a clean flat pottery dish, a beautiful piece of crystal, a small polished copper bowl and a wooden box.

"Do you smoke?" he asked, surprised. He had never smelled tobacco on her.

"No. That was my father's pipe."

Power emanated from the box. He glanced at Xanthe who hovered nearby, watching him closely. "May I?"

She took a deep breath, her fingers twisted together, and nodded.

He lifted the box up, handling it with care, and examined it from all sides before he opened it to look at the deck of cards inside. "There's a tale to tell here."

"I got it from Duncan and Seremela," she told him. "Seremela's niece had stolen it, and they didn't want to be responsible for it. I said—I said I would take care of it."

"Did you?" He turned over the first exquisitely crafted card and looked upon the fierce, golden face of Love. Then he turned over the second card to look at the sharp, ruthless visage of Law. "These cards are really quite extraordinary. You don't have any clue as to their origins?"

She shook her head. "I think—I think the right thing to do is to take them to one of the gods' shrines," she said softly.

He raised his eyebrows. Her voice was filled with something complex, but he could not decipher what it was. He set the cards carefully back in the box, closed the lid and set the box respectfully back onto the mantel.

"I am no expert in items of Power, but if you are unsure about these, then offering them to the gods at one of the shrines would be appropriate." He turned to put his hand on her shoulder, spreading his fingers over the finely sculpted shape of it, gently rubbing her through the soft cloth of her tunic. Giving in to temptation, he said quietly, "I have a very selfish desire to fall asleep listening to your voice. Can I coax you into reading to me for a little while?"

She swallowed and told him huskily, "I would be glad to."

His conscience stirred and grumbled. She had done so much for him already. He squashed it, choosing the selfish act, choosing to explore everything he could with her. He wanted to hear her voice. She had agreed. Experience told him that she certainly knew how to say no. He could not both hunt her and simultaneously protect her from himself.

He walked into the shadowed bedroom, drew off his robe and laid it at the foot of the bed, and slid naked between the sheets. As the cool linen slid across his skin, an image came to him of Xanthe, spread underneath his body, her face tilted up in agonized pleasure, and as tired as he was, his penis stiffened again and throbbed with urgency.

He ignored it. Now was not the time to act. As disconcerted as Xanthe had shown herself to be over the attraction that grew between them, he suspected it was too soon for her. He did not want to initiate anything prematurely. They each deserved better.

A chair scraped across the floor. He called out, "Why don't you leave it? There is more than enough room for you to sit on the bed."

A pause, then she said, "Very well."

He lit the lantern on the bedside table while she shut and bolted the cottage door. By the time she stepped into the room, he lay back on the pillows with the covers pulled up to his chest. He watched her from underneath lowered eyelids as she moved to the pile of books. Her long body moved with a grace that caught at his throat. He longed to touch her with reverence and tell her how much she was coming to mean to him.

"Which book would you like for me to read?" she asked.

"I don't care," he told her. "Why don't you pick one that you're interested in?"

"All right." She hesitated then chose a Dark Fae story and settled on one corner of the bed, leaning back against the headboard with one leg bent and tucked underneath her.

He closed his eyes as she began to read. The liquid notes of her voice filled the room, shaping words that created a story, but he did not care about that. He merely listened to the sound of her voice, the intonation and inflection, and the cadence she gave to each sentence, as if he was listening to a solo musician. It was incredibly soothing.

She halted, faltering into silence, as he turned onto his side and nuzzled her thigh, resting one relaxed hand on her knee. He refused to pull away or regret the move, and after a pause she resumed the story, her voice much softer.

After a few moments more, a light, gentle weight came down on the back of his head. She rested her hand on him as she read.

Naida had not been affectionate. They had maintained separate bedrooms, coming together for sex but never sleeping in the same bed. He had accepted that about her. Some people simply weren't.

He was affectionate.

He smiled and slipped into a doze.

Sometime later, he roused as the bed shifted and Xanthe began to ease away. Without really thinking about it, he tightened his hand on her knee, murmuring, "Stay."

She drew in a quick breath, the slight sound seemed loud in the silence of the bedroom. She said softly, "I thought you had fallen asleep."

"I did. You moved." His voice was gravelly.

"I'm sorry I woke you."

He yawned and rolled onto his back, then opened his eyes to look at her. She wore an uncertain, vulnerable expression that squeezed at his chest. She would never be one for the cynical dalliances that the nobility indulged in. He lifted his hand to her, she took it and he pressed her fingers.

He told her quietly, "The bed is large, and there is more than enough room for two. You could even sleep with the covers between us if you like. No matter what you may have been used to in the past, I would feel better knowing that you weren't on the cold hard floor, but it is entirely up to you. I don't want you to be uncomfortable in any way."

She was silent for so long. As he waited, he urged her, *do it. Choose to do what you really want.*

At last she whispered, "I'll stay."

Tension had gathered in his limbs as he waited for her to decide. At her words it released, leaving a lingering lightness that felt like joy. He slid over as she shrugged out of her trousers, revealing long, gorgeous pale legs. Without looking at him, she lifted the top quilt and slipped into bed, leaving the sheet and a cotton blanket as a privacy barrier between them. The last thing she did was blow out the lamp before she settled with a sigh.

He kept his breathing soft and even, even as desire flooded his body.

Then she said in entirely prosaic exasperation, "Rats. We should have eaten up the rest of the clotted cream at supper, and I forgot all about it."

He lay frozen for a moment, all thought suspended. When he burst out laughing, she chuckled too.

He rolled over, and despite the barrier between them, he pulled her into his arms and hugged her. She came willingly, fitting herself to him, one arm tucked around him as he guided her head onto his shoulder. He pressed his lips to her forehead, lingering over the caress and stroked her still damp hair. She nuzzled at his bare shoulder, breathing deeply as she settled and, muscle by muscle, relaxed.

Holding her gave him a feeling of incredible rightness, comfort and relief. When he slept, for the first time in a very long time, there was no pain.

When he opened his eyes again, it was full morning and he was alone. Disappointed, he laid a hand on the pillow she had used. It was still warm. She had only just left the bed.

His body had the memory of holding Xanthe through the night. At one point, she curled onto her side and he moved too, curling behind her to spoon with her, one arm wrapped around her waist. She had laced her fingers through his as he buried his nose in her soft, silken hair.

Now she moved around in the other room. The quiet sounds were already comforting and familiar. Cautiously he tried a full body stretch. The muscles in his back still gave a twinge, but the warning no longer seemed filled with dire consequences. He should start some exercises today.

He rose out of bed, reveling in the sense of his returning strength, and slipped on a clean pair of trousers. Then he left the bedroom to commence stalking the woman he meant to make his lover.

She knelt at the hearth, laying wood for a morning fire. Her hair was loose and tousled, and her cheek was creased from the pillow linens—and there, it happened again. She had grown even more beautiful to him.

I'm falling in love with you, he thought. *And damn, it's a deep, deep fall.*

Falling in love with her wasn't a decision; it was a full mind-body, transformative experience. Backing away, choosing not to explore the opportunity—that would the decision. And he wasn't about to throw any of this away. It was too rare, too enriching. She was too fine of a treasure to be so disregarded.

Besides, he hungered for her, for everything she was. For her dedication and loyalty, for the sensuality of her long, lithe body, for the fullness of emotion he caught shimmering in her eyes when she looked at him.

She straightened and pushed the hair out of her face in a self-conscious gesture as he walked over to her. He pulled her into his arms, tilted up her face and kissed her. Not a quick kiss this time, but a slow, searching explorative caress.

His lips remembered the shape of hers and were eager to mold to them again, while his heart thundered and his entire body hardened, and he felt immersed in a coursing river of emotion, in her. Breathing deeply, he fisted one hand in her hair, wanting to deepen the kiss but waiting for some kind of sign.

Kiss me. Kiss me back.

Her arms came around him, hands flattening greedily against his back even as she pulled her head away. She muttered, "We shouldn't be doing this—"

He flashed back fiercely, "Fuck that."

He never cursed. The shock of it bolted across her face. Then he realized how tightly his hand had clenched in her hair. He willed himself to pry his fingers open, to loosen his hold and stroke her hair gently. His hand was unsteady.

She stared at him, her gaze clear open down to the bottom of her soul.

"Xanthe," he said between his teeth as a horrible thought occurred to him. "Have you made promises to someone else?"

Her expression turned even more shocked. "No!"

"Then if you say a word about me being the Chancellor or you being a guard, I might just throttle you. There is no place for that here, between us. I am just a man who wants to kiss you. Do you want to kiss me back? That is the only consideration of any relevance in this moment. If you do not, just say so and I'm sorry I assumed too much—"

She lunged up on tiptoe, her arms snaking around his neck, and kissed him hard.

There it was, what he had been looking for, her full-bodied, full-hearted cooperation. He closed his eyes and sank into her mouth, spearing into her as deeply as he could go.

What they created together was a wild storm of emotion. This time when she pulled back, she was shaking all over.

He loved that.

"Okay," she whispered. "Okay."

He was not prepared to let her off the hook. He cupped the nape of her neck, holding her in place as he leaned his forehead on hers. He said in a low voice, "You will stay in the bed again with me tonight."

She licked her lips and said, "Yes."

He pressed her further, one hand gripping her hip. "And there will not be a sheet or a blanket between us."

Her dark gaze searched his. Her eyes were such a lovely, deep color, filled with clarity, intelligence and depth. "No blankets, Aubrey." Her fingertips stroked over his lips. "Except for the ones we pull over us both."

He released a long, pent-up breath and pressed a kiss against her fingers.

She shook her head. "You have knocked everything sensible outside of my head again. I think I was starting to fix breakfast."

He purred, "We could always go back to bed right now."

She lost all of her composure again. "I—you—seriously?"

He laughed, a throaty, delighted sound. She sounded almost panicked at the thought. "Forget about breakfast, or even bed right now. Why don't we step outside for some fresh air. We could even go for a walk. The river is close, isn't it?"

She took a step back to eye him, her gaze turning assessing. She smiled. "You're really doing better."

He nodded. "I'm still stiff, especially in my back. But it's much better now."

"An oiled massage would help with a lot of that stiffness."

That demon of lunacy took over his tongue. He said, deadpan, "I think an oiled massage would take care of all kinds of stiffness."

Hot color washed over her cheeks. She added, strangled, "Certainly, that is, if you—think you might—I meant especially on that wound on your back to loosen up the muscles."

He shouted with laughter. "By all the gods, woman, how did you survive in the army for so long?"

Her embarrassment turned into a glare. "I'm not like this with anybody else!"

His laughter faded. Warmed, he cupped her cheek and rubbed his thumb over those soft, unusually full lips. "Really?"

She nodded dumbly.

"I cherish all of it," he whispered.

Clearly she was not used to compliments, for she showed none of the polished deflection practiced by so many of the ladies of his acquaintance. Every word he said affected her deeply; he could see it in her eyes.

She was an assassin, and she had survived not only in Urien's palace for decades, but she had also survived Thruvial's household. Yet with him, she did not barrier any part of herself or use the many tools that must exist in her repertoire. Instead she revealed to him a heart of glass, fragile and beautifully faceted in every way, luminous with light.

He could not remember ever feeling so touched, or so honored.

"Come," she said. "I'll show you my favorite spot by the river. We can even fish if you want. I like fish for breakfast."

"So do I," he told her.

He got dressed fully, pulling on a shirt and boots. The day was fine enough again that no jacket was necessary. He tied his hair back with the leather strip, and splashed his face with water from the basin.

She had braided back her hair and gathered a basket of fishing supplies from a bottom shelf. As soon as he gave her a nod, she lifted her sword and harness from the hook by the door, although she did not bother to shrug it on.

He took the basket so it would free one of her hands then he captured it with his own, lacing his fingers through hers. Giving him a gleaming, bright smile, she led him on a pleasant walk to the river.

Their route bisected a large path that was more of a small road that followed the river's length. Now that he knew where the river was, he knew the path would lead to Adriyel, but he no longer cared to follow it. They settled in the shade of a massive oak tree.

Adriyel was the great river in the Dark Fae land. It poured hundreds of leagues through the heart of the land. The bank on the opposite side was certainly visible, but the details were obscured in the distance. It was treacherous to swim the long length from one side to the other, but every year some fools attempted it. Many were swept downstream and drowned.

Here, down a steep bank from the oak, there was an indentation with a relatively shallow pool. Smiling, she pointed down to it. "This was my favorite place in the heat of the summer, although my father never took his eyes off of me for a moment, for fear I would forget and get too close to the river's current."

"This must have been a great place to play as a child," he said.

"It was. We were happy." She lifted a shoulder. "I remember us being happy, at any rate. I'm sure he missed my mother, but she died in childbirth with me, so I never knew her. He was my only parent as a child growing up."

That would have made losing him especially hard for her. Dark Fae could live for a very long time, but there were still accidents, war and certain diseases that could claim lives. Long, long ago, his own parents had been taken in a virulent epidemic that had swept through their home seat in the country.

She sprawled with her long legs crossed at the ankle. He braced himself against the trunk of the oak to go through a round of stretching exercises. She watched closely, and offered some suggestions. Afterward, he lay beside her on the thick, rich grass of the bank, hands laced behind his neck as they talked.

Neither bothered to reach for the fishing basket. They were too focused on each other to care. The sunlight turned the green oak leaves golden, and a fresh cool breeze blew off river. Sexual arousal and affection blanketed them together in warmth and comfort, and imbued him with a sense of wellbeing.

They both heard the voices at the same time.

Male voices, approaching in their direction.

"It must be around here somewhere," said one. "This is the area they said. Just a bit further, maybe around that bend."

"Well, we've got to continue," said another. "There's no going back now."

Even as Aubrey sat up, Xanthe threw herself on him, one hand clamped over his mouth. She stared into his eyes, her own gaze sharp and steady.

"Don't make a sound", she told him telepathically.

He nodded as he clasped her wrist. *"I understand."*

"I am going to check where they are." She rolled off of him and to her feet in one silent, lithe movement, scooping up her sword and harness as she rose. She shrugged it on quickly, her expression as keen as the blade that settled between her shoulders. She glanced down at him and touched a finger to her lips. He nodded again, and she disappeared through the waist high grass that bordered the path.

He rolled to his feet, not nearly as gracefully as she, as his wretched back muscles threatened to seize up again. After a second's consideration, he snatched up the fishing basket, not because the contents mattered so much as leaving it on the bank would have given away their presence. When he noticed the indentation their bodies had made in the grass, he wiped the area back and forth with one boot until the marks were gone.

By then Xanthe was back. She had drawn her sword. She gestured to him with her free hand. *"Come on, we must go this way."*

She led him on a different, more difficult route than they had taken earlier, further upstream for a while before they cut back across the path, and through a tangled, overgrown thicket, until finally they arrived back at the cottage.

As soon as they stepped inside, she grabbed her wrist guards that held throwing knives and began to strap them on.

"I need to follow them and discover what they're up to," she said, in a rapid, quiet voice. "It's possible their presence doesn't have anything to do with us, but we need to know if they're hunting you. As soon as I leave, I want you to bolt the door and the windows. Don't answer if anyone knocks. There are the kitchen knives if you need weapons. I'll return as fast as I can."

"Don't do this," he said. He grabbed her by the shoulders.

She stared at him as if he were crazy. "I have to."

"Then I'll come with you." He glared around the cottage. "Gods damn it, there's only one sword."

"Of course there's only one sword. You are not yet healed enough to face another fight."

"No one will refrain from attacking me because I'm not yet healed enough to face it," he snapped. "I can hold my own if I have to."

"Aubrey, listen to me." Her face was fierce. "In this one thing there is no equity between us. There is only one person in the world like you, and there are dozens like me. You are the Chancellor. I am your guard. I swear to you, I will be back."

Her words struck him like individual blows. He grabbed her and spun her around to face him, his fingers digging into her shoulders.

"No, you listen to me," he said between his teeth. "I will not let you go out there alone. I will not remain tamely in this cottage and wait for you, without knowing whether or not you are all right, or if you may have been killed. There is no one else in the world like you, and I will not run the risk of losing you just after I found you. We go together or we stay here. Together. Either way, you choose, but that's the only choice you're going to get."

Chapter Seven

Love

S he stared up at him, mesmerized by the taut emotion that transformed his expression and clenched his long body. His hands felt hard as iron as his fingers dug into her shoulders, but she paid no attention to the discomfort. All she could do was hear the echo of his words resounding in her head.

"There is no one else in the world like you."

"I will not run the risk of losing you just after I found you."

He sounded—he sounded like he might—

By sheer force of will, she yanked herself back to the only thing that was relevant. She hissed, "I will not let anyone hurt you again, ever."

He said, "You said yourself their presence probably doesn't have anything to do with us. And if they are hunting for us, they will find the cottage soon enough."

"Not if I find them first." She raised her hands and tried to knock away his hold, but she refused to strike him hard, and he refused to let go of her. "If they are hunting for you—if they find the cottage, they can pin us in here."

He shook her, not hard but tightly enough to snap her attention back to his face. "Stop reacting and think," he said, still in that harsh-edged voice. "Nobody knows I'm here, just you, Tiago and Niniane and they would never breathe a word to anyone, yes?"

Her breath came hard. After a moment, she said, "Yes."

Although his features had calmed somewhat, the tension had not left his body. He pushed her backward until she came up against the wall. He said softly, "So the only way anyone could possibly think to look here is through the wildest chance that either Tiago or Niniane let slip some very specific information. Yes?"

She didn't know where he was going with this, but she was pretty sure she didn't like it. She snapped, "Yes."

He pushed his body against hers and rested his forearms on the wall on either side of her head, pinning her. Then he put his forehead to hers.

If he had been an enemy, she knew exactly what she would do to get away. A knee to the groin and a hard clip over the head with both hands locked together. That would buy her enough space and time to draw her sword.

But he wasn't the enemy. He was the dearest thing in the world to her. Even the thought of doing violence to him caused her to feel slightly queasy.

"I'm willing to take that wildest chance and stay here with you," he said. "I am not willing to take that wildest chance and let you go alone into a situation that might be deadly for you."

Somehow her arms ended up around his waist. She held him in a clinch. "I cannot stay safe and guard you at the same time."

"You're fired," he said immediately. He lowered his head and nuzzled her.

She felt like she was nearly leaping out of her skin with so many conflicting impulses. "You can't fire me." Her voice was all over the place, wildly unsteady. "I don't work for you."

"I am close friends with your employers. You're fired as soon as they come back." His lips brushed her cheek. "Xanthe, stay with me."

She took fistfuls of his shirt, feeling the broad, tight muscles underneath. "I am not willing to take the wildest chance on your safety and wellbeing either."

"I know, darling." He kissed the indentation at the corner of her mouth. "Everything you have done for days has been for my best good." He lifted his head slightly. His expression had turned tender. "No one has ever cared for me like you have."

"No one ever will." The words escaped her; they just escaped her, barely audible and yet laying her soul wide open.

He tilted his head and covered her mouth hard with his, a strong, confident taking that pushed her head back against the wall. Her legs shook; she felt drenched with erotic shock as he deepened the kiss, pushing into her mouth with his tongue. She could barely breathe and couldn't think. Her body's instincts took over and she kissed him back wildly.

His hardened lips slid over hers, slick with their moisture. Her heart was pounding so that she thought it might burst from her chest. She was almost lost, almost—

But no. Decades of training asserted itself.

She yanked her mouth away and gasped, "I need to know where those men went."

He was breathing as heavily as she was, his entire body run through with the finest tremor. He stared at her mouth, his darkened gaze sensual and compulsive. For a moment she thought he would refuse to lift his body weight from hers. Then with a grimace, he pulled back. "All right. We go together."

She didn't try to argue anymore—with their last fierce exchange they had catapulted each other into a strange new realm where she didn't understand the rules. Instead she shrugged out of her harness and tried to hand her sword to him. "Take this. I'll take the knives."

He stared down at the sword in her hand without moving to take it. Then he gave her a quirk of a smile. "When I am up to speed, I am a perfectly good swordsman. But I am not at my best, and you have to be one of the finest in the army for Tiago to agree to you becoming one of Niniane's guards. You keep the sword. I'll take the knives."

She scowled, not liking either possibility for how they divided the weapons. But she strapped the harness back on again, while he took her wrist guards with the knives. Then they slipped quietly out of the cottage, into the growing heat of the day.

Sunshine pressed down heavily, the silence broken with the occasional call from birds and the heavy drone of insects. Aubrey gestured for her to lead the way, and she took them in a wide circle that circumvented the cottage. Having found no sign of the men, they moved wider afield until they checked the path where the men had been before. Then finally they moved to the bank of the river. She was studying the bank for footprints when Aubrey nudged her gently and pointed downstream.

She glanced where he pointed. Some distance away the riverbank jutted out in a small promontory that was little more than a tangled mass of tree trunks and debris that had been swept downstream. A small barge had gotten tangled in the debris, and two men, covered in mud, were working to get it loose.

The knot of tension that had tightened her shoulders loosened.

Aubrey slipped an arm around her shoulders from behind, his forearm crossing at her collarbones. He pulled her back against him and said in her ear, "Looks like someone's livelihood might have slipped its mooring and floated downstream. Satisfied?"

She nodded, letting her head fall back against his shoulder. After a moment, she said, "I'm not sorry for being so paranoid. You really did almost die."

He heaved a rough sigh. "I know."

His body felt hot and tense. Her mind was split wide open with incredulity for this blaze of fire that had leapt up between them.

"There is no one else in the world like you. I'm willing to take that wildest chance and stay here with you."

He cupped her neck with one hand while he kissed the sensitive shell of her ear and whispered, "Let's go home."

Home? The sound of that word, coming from him, gave her another thrill of shock. Unable to form words, she nodded. His arm loosened and he let her go.

They made short work of the trip back to the cottage. Once there, she shrugged out of her harness and hung her sword on its hook. Aubrey gazed at her steadily while he yanked open the fastenings on the wrist guards. Her mind hazed with heat. Desire for this man was the sweetest pain she had ever known. That he might grow to want her too was beyond anything she could have dreamed of, extraordinary.

In fact it was hardly believable.

The thought drove her across the room, away from him. She wrapped her arms around her middle, chewing on her lip as she looked guiltily at the box on the fireplace mantle. His slow, measured tread came up behind her; she was so hyperaware of him, she knew to the exact moment when his hands would come down on her shoulders.

"What's wrong?" he asked quietly.

The question burst out of her. "Do you think the gods can make us do things we wouldn't otherwise do?"

His thumbs rubbed soothingly at her shoulder blades. "Why do you ask?"

Her body was trembling with the force of her own desire to keep silent, to take what he offered her with his hands and his mouth. But she couldn't.

She whispered, "When Dr. Telemar—the medusa—couldn't identify what kind of Power was in those Tarot cards, I started to wonder about those old legends about the gods putting items in the world to enact their will. Inanna's card keeps surfacing. If the cards are hers—could they be influencing us to act in ways we might not otherwise act?"

He was silent for a long, thoughtful moment. Then he brushed her braid aside and pressed a kiss to the nape of her neck. "The chances of such a thing would be outrageously rare, you know," he said gently. "And while the good Dr. Telemar is no doubt highly proficient at her job, she is but one physician and the world is filled with many strange and different magics."

"I know," she whispered.

He pulled her into his arms. "Even if we were so lucky to have an item of Inanna's working in our lives, no, I do not believe the gods can or would make us act against our natures or inclinations. Our free will is one of the primal Powers after all. Inanna may give us the opportunity for love, but it's our choice whether or not we take that opportunity, and love is what we make of it."

She said in a low voice, "I just find it hard to believe that you might—you might want me."

He turned her around and stared into her eyes. "Xanthe, you are the most beautiful surprise in my life. I hardly noticed you at first. You carry the quiet of a river with a still surface that runs very deep. I found that the more I looked at you, the more I saw—and now the more I see of you, the more beautiful you become and the more I want you." He paused then said deeply, "I've never wanted anyone the way I have grown to want you."

Her trembling deepened as she listened to him. Overcome, she laid her hand against his lean cheek. "Me neither."

He smiled at her, slow and intimate, as his hands drifted gently, gently to the front of her shirt. He gave her plenty of time to say something, to object or pull away, as he teased open the top button, then a second one. Her breathing quickened as she watched his long, clever fingers work the material open. When she glanced up at him, she saw that his breathing had quickened also.

Her shirt came unfastened and he pulled the edges open, gazing down at her breasts. She was slim everywhere, muscles sleek and strong under pale, smooth skin. Her breasts were high and slight, the pale pink nipples pebbling in the open air.

He touched the swelling, velvet soft skin of her breast with shaking, gentle hands, and brushed the extremely sensitive jut of one nipple with the back of his fingers. Sensation and emotion coursed through her, the small pleasure brought to an extreme by the awareness that he was the one who touched her with such care.

She looked up at his dear face, both noble and kind, and surprised an expression of vulnerability. He said, very low, "I have not been with anyone since my wife died. I felt dead inside for so long."

Compassion wrenched her. She circled his wrists loosely with her hands. "We don't have to do this, Aubrey, if you're not ready."

"Yes, we do." His eyes blazed. "She took so much from me. I will not lose any more of my life to her. For a long time, I didn't see how I could learn to trust someone again. Until you."

Tears burned at the back of her eyes. "I would never hurt you. Never. I'll kill anyone who tries."

His clenched expression softened into a tender smile. He cupped her face and whispered, "I believe you."

She pulled his hair loose from the tie that held it back, and the long raven strands fell about his lean face as he bent his head to kiss her. Starting out light and tender, the caress rapidly escalated until he gripped the back of her head and dug, groaning, into her open, inviting mouth.

Need for him throbbed low in her body. She pulled at his shirt until the buttons scattered across the floor then ran her hands hungrily across his hard, lean chest. He snaked an arm around her and yanked her against him, until they were hip to hip. As she felt the full length of his erection against her pelvis, she made an animal noise and rubbed against him.

Still kissing her, he pushed her, back and back, and she obeyed blindly until she came up against the table. He nudged her to sit and he tore off the rest of her clothes while she yanked his trousers open and reached greedily for his penis. It was hard, thick and beautifully made, silken skin stretched over stiffened flesh. Staring at his face, she fingered the length of his cock and stroked him, while he closed his eyes and swallowed hard. He pushed at her hands with his hips, and she pumped him slowly, losing herself in the moment of giving him pleasure.

His voice turned guttural, he said, "Stop."

She muttered a protest as he pulled out of her grip, and she reached for him again, but he brushed her seeking hands out of the way and pushed her back onto the table. Once she understood what he wanted, she lay back, her spine arched and torso stretched out on display for him as her legs spilled over the edge.

He froze, one hand planted on the table beside her waist, breathing hard as he stared down at her. Some strong emotion played over his face. Worried, she reached up to touch his lips. "What is it?"

He whispered from the back of his throat, "It just happened again. You're even lovelier than ever."

She could tell there was no barrier in him anywhere. He looked at her, totally bared and open, and she knew what he meant, for he had never looked so beautiful to her. She murmured, "Come inside."

He shook his head. "Not yet. Soon."

He came down over her, resting his weight on his elbows as he traced the line of her collarbone with his tongue. His heartbeat thudded hard and fast against her breast. She hooked her heels on the on the edge of the table, cradling him between her legs and murmuring incoherently as she stroked his hair. It was impossible to love him more than she did, impossible. Tears slipped from the corners of her eyes and soaked into her hair as he worked his way down to her breasts. Eyes closed, he suckled first at one nipple then the other, teasing her sensitive flesh lightly and then drawing hard, so that her clitoris throbbed in agonizing response and she cried out, clawing at his shoulders in urgent, wordless demand.

Still suckling, he worked one hand between their bodies and fingered the soft petals of her sex, drawing out moisture and rubbing his cock against her. She was so slick with arousal, she felt the wetness coating him.

He pushed steady and gentle until the thick, broad head of his penis slipped in, and he stopped just long enough that she pulled at his hair and sobbed out, "Don't tease me right now."

At that he threw back his head. His face was twisted; he looked transformed, outside of himself. A growl wrenched out of him, and in one convulsive move he sheathed himself inside of her.

In, in, in, he was all the way in. She cried out, gripping him tightly with her inner muscles, while she raised her legs and wrapped them around his torso.

His hoarse, panting breath was like a bellows in her ear, and his long hair covered her face. He shook all over. She hugged him with her whole body and soul, fiercely, stroking the back of his head with one hand while she rubbed his back.

"Tell me you're all right," she whispered, growing anxious as he held so still.

Tell me you won't regret this.

He looked down at her and smiled, his face filled with tenderness and sharp passion. He said, "I've never been better. You feel like a wet silk fist. Gods— Xanthe—"

She tightened on him harder as he slid out, and he shuddered hard and drove back in. He pulled out again, excruciatingly slow. Unable to wait, she mewled and thrust her hips up, impaling herself on him. His big body jerked as he gasped. He put a hand between them again; she felt him probing for her clitoris as he fucked her. Something came out of her mouth, an uncontrolled string of words. She had no idea what she said. She was on fire everywhere, everywhere. It blazed from the point of his entry, the unbearably gorgeous pressure of his fingers on exactly the right place.

"Oh shit," he said.

He twisted in her arms. Inside, she felt him begin to pulse as he lost control. Then that desire, that sweetest pain she felt for no one but him, peaked like a starburst. She cried out as her own climax rippled through her. He ground against her, shuddering.

Silence, their passion released. She cradled him as he rested his forehead on her shoulder. The table was uncomfortably hard on her spine, and she would not have moved for the world. With her fingers, she circled the slight knob of bone at the base of his nape and traced what she could reach of the long line of scar across his back, soaking up every sensual piece of evidence she could get of him.

I'll not ever forget this moment, she thought. *Not ever, not even if I live for a very, very long time.*

Eventually the discomfort of his position forced him to move. He pushed himself up on one hand, wincing as his back muscles seized up in protest and his softened penis slid out of her.

"Well, this is inelegant," he said through gritted teeth.

The gorgeous dazed look left her face, and she laughed, her gaze sympathetic. "It's that damn wound on your back, isn't it?"

He nodded. Limber and graceful, she slid out from underneath him and rolled off the table. When she was upright, she slipped under his arm and took his weight, helping him to straighten. He forced himself to take a deep breath. Then he kissed her.

She murmured, and he drew her close, relishing the feel of her naked body against his. At last, with obvious reluctance, she pulled away. "Let me get the vial of oil," she said. "You need a back massage to loosen those muscles, especially after the stretching exercises from earlier and—you know." Unexpectedly, her face turned dark red.

"I won't say no," he said. He stroked her cheek, inexpressibly delighted at the blush. Delighted with everything about her. "Xanthe, I love you."

She grew very still, her eyes, full of that great, shining heart of glass, fixed on him. When she made as if to say something, he touched her lips with two fingers and shook his head with a smile. Just because he felt the need to tell her how he felt didn't mean that she should feel the need to reciprocate.

He went into the other room and eased down onto the bed to lay on his aching back with a muffled groan. A few moments later, she joined him.

He loved watching her walk across the room nude. Her breasts were reddened by his attention, and the black silken triangle between her legs glistened with moisture. Her body was sleek and powerful, like a panther's, and despite the shyness she had shown to him in various other ways, she had no body shyness at all and she moved with complete, athletic confidence that he found incredibly sexy. His cock stirred as he watched her; he was so hungry for her, he was already beginning to stiffen again.

She had gathered up their clothes and she set them on the floor by the bed. Then she took a small vial of oil and poured some into the palm of her hand. Her gaze flew involuntarily to his groin, and he clenched his teeth on another laugh as she flushed pink all over.

"Oh gods, please do," he growled.

She scolded, "I'm supposed to rub your back!"

He loved it when she scolded him. He grasped her knee, gently. "My back is perfectly fine while I'm lying down. It can wait. It's everything else that feels urgent right now."

She looked at him, stricken laughter in her gaze, and he could see that she was tempted.

"After we work on your muscles a bit."

He gave her a lazy, one-sided, calculating smile. "Very well, but I won't roll over until you give me a kiss."

He watched her gaze grow heavy lidded, and his cock stiffened further. "All right."

She bent over him, her mouth softened, and he raised his head to meet her, kissing her lavishly, feeling hunger for her roar to a fever pitch all over again. When she would have pulled away, he grabbed her and yanked her back down, so that she overbalanced and fell on him.

Instinctively she caught herself on his chest, bracing on the hand that had held the palm full of oil. The warm liquid splashed across his torso as her slippery hand slid off his skin, and she sprawled on top of him.

He growled deeper, an arm wrapped around her neck as he plunged hectically between her lips. While he fucked her mouth with his tongue, he rubbed his chest with a hand until it was slick with oil, then he palmed her breast, that high, firm luscious mound of flesh. She moaned, the shaken sound vibrating in his mouth.

The oiled, slick friction of their bodies drove him out of his mind. He bit her neck, suckled at her ear, sank both fists into her hair and muttered, "Climb on top."

The glazed look was back in her eyes, arousal shimmering out of her flesh in waves of velvet heat. He held her by the hair down to him, while she straddled his hips with hers. She groped for his cock blindly; when she took hold of him, she brought his tip to her entrance and sank down, down, sheathing him again in that tight, wet fist.

She was off balance, bent over, her weight on her elbows, but he could not seem to make his fingers loosen from her hair. It was uncivilized, possessive in the extreme. It was either unlike him or it was the truest manifestation of who he was becoming with her.

He hissed against her lips, "Fuck me, just like this."

She groaned and obeyed, her hips moving on him in a primitive rhythm that he met with upward thrusts, spearing into her with cock and tongue, blind to everything but the need to enter her, enter her. She sobbed for breath, the jagged puffs of breath against his face as erotic as anything they had done together.

Her face was reddened; tears streaked her eyes, and strands of her hair were plastered to her damp face and neck. "Gorgeous, gorgeous," he said into her mouth. "You gorgeous woman."

At that she gave a sharp cry, her whole body going taut as a bow, and he felt the ripple of her orgasm deep inside of her as she clenched on him. It sent him over the edge. He slid a hand down to her ass, pressing her down hard as he ejaculated deep inside of her. It satisfied everything primal inside of him.

The world pulsed with their heartbeats, their sweating bodies fused together. She lay across him, her head resting on his chest. Finally he was able to loosen his grip on her hair. He pushed the strands back from her face and tried to smooth the tangles out.

"I've loved you for a very long time," she said. Her voice was very soft, almost inaudible. He stilled, straining to hear every word. "Of course mostly that was hero worship and not very realistic."

"I'm no hero," he said.

She snorted softly. "You're a hero to everyone, Aubrey. Just not to yourself." He frowned, but she was continuing. "Then I got to know you better. The real you. The real, cranky, kind, funny you. Gods help me."

He cupped her face. "Why do you need the gods to help you, darling?"

Her eyes were closed. She whispered, "We'll be going back to our lives soon enough."

His frown deepened. "Xanthe," he said tightly. "I don't know what this is for you, but this is not just an interlude for me. Yes, our time here at the cottage is outside the boundaries of normality, and yes, we have our jobs and duties waiting for us back in the city, but I am living an authentic life—who I am here is who I am back there too. I said I love you. I didn't say it because we just had sex. I said it because I love you. You had better tell me if you don't want to see me when we get back—and even then I'll try to persuade you otherwise—"

She rose up and kissed him quickly. "No, that's not what I meant! I—I didn't want to presume anything just because we—we—you know." She made a gesture that encompassed them and the bed.

His tightness eased. He smiled at her. "Please presume all the 'you knows' that you want. I strongly encourage all kinds of presuming from you."

That startled her into a grin. As she opened her mouth to say something—

They heard voices approaching the cottage: Niniane's and Tiago's.

Panic flashed across Xanthe's face. She rolled off the bed and peered out the window. "We didn't shut the cottage door," she muttered. She flew at her clothes.

While she yanked on her shirt and trousers, Aubrey rolled off the bed. He strolled over to the bedroom door to shut it firmly.

Just outside the cottage, Niniane called, "Hello, Aubrey? Xanthe? Are you here?"

He called out, "We're here, but we're not dressed. Give us a minute, and we'll be right out."

Silence. Then: "Okay."

He turned to Xanthe. "Darling, don't panic," he whispered. "Take your time."

"She's only the Queen," Xanthe hissed. She dragged her fingers frantically through her hair and braided it. Apparently it wasn't straight enough to satisfy her, so she yanked it out and did it again. "And she's my employer. Oh holy gods, Tiago's out there."

He started to laugh as he dressed. When he slipped on his shirt, he couldn't find any buttons, so he left it open. Xanthe was still trying to get her hair into a plait when he opened the door and walked out.

Tiago stood in the doorway, facing the outside, arms crossed and harsh profile expressionless. Niniane stood by the table, unpacking canvas bags of supplies. She did not look expressionless. Her small, piquant face was full of suppressed glee.

"Hello," Aubrey said. "How are you today?"

"We are quite well," Niniane said. Her eyes danced. "You are looking so much better, Aubrey."

"I'm feeling better than I have in a long time," he told her, as he pressed a kiss to her cheek. He whispered, "Xanthe is in a panic. Tell Tiago to be nice or I will hurt him."

"Oh, he'll be nice," Niniane whispered back. "Or if he can't manage nice, he'll be silent if he knows what's good for him."

"I know what's good for me," Tiago said to the general out of doors.

Xanthe appeared, her back ramrod stiff. Her clothes were as neat as she could make them, and her braid was not quite immaculate, but really quite well done given the circumstances. She murmured, "Your grace, sir."

She was almost, but not quite, perfectly expressionless. Aubrey couldn't stand it. He walked over to her and put an arm around her. She just looked at him, her lips white. He was not altogether convinced that she was breathing.

We need to rip this bandage off right now, he thought. He said aloud, "Xanthe and I have just decided to continue seeing each other when we return to the city. We don't need your blessing, but we would very much appreciate it."

"Of course you have it," Niniane said immediately. She gave Xanthe a warm smile. "I couldn't be more delighted. I really mean that, Xanthe."

Aubrey felt the tension in Xanthe's shoulders ease, although she glanced at Tiago again. He did too. Tiago's eyebrows had raised, but other than that, for all intents and purposes he appeared to be watching birds.

"How is the investigation going?" Aubrey asked.

Tiago looked over one massive shoulder at Niniane who nodded. The Wyr lord said, "The investigation was over within twenty-four hours of your attack, with all arrests made."

At first the words didn't make sense. His arm fell from Xanthe's shoulders and he ran his fingers through his hair. "Wait a minute," he said. More like growled. "That would mean everything was over with the first time you came with supplies."

"That is correct," said Tiago.

Xanthe strode forward quickly, "Who did it?"

"Naida's father, Grove Ealdun, was behind it," Tiago said. "We have the people he hired too." He met Aubrey's gaze. "Your secretary, Sebrin, is a little battered around the edges but all right. Sebrin gave himself away when he went digging. Ealdun had captured him but hadn't yet killed him. When he realized you were responsible for sending Sebrin, he tried to have you killed, in part for revenge. In part, too, because he thought you were going to try to have him prosecuted for the false evidence. The ironic thing is that I don't think any of us would have bothered with prosecuting for the false evidence, but now of course it's attempted murder. The whole thing was pretty simple and straight-forward, in a Dark Fae kind of way."

"You said there were complications," Aubrey snapped. He glared at Niniane, "You ordered me to stay here."

Niniane bit her thumbnail. She looked worried as she replied, "Neither one of us said there were complications with the investigation, Aubrey. We only said that there were complications."

"What does that mean?" he roared, fists on his hips.

Tiago gave him a warning look, but he ignored it.

Niniane gave Xanthe an apologetic glance then said to him, "The night you were almost killed, I—saw something, Aubrey. I saw just how much you meant to Xanthe. So when Tiago tore through the investigation in record time, and he threw everybody in prison, well—you were here at the cottage anyway, so we just left you. This last year has been so hard on you both, each for your own reasons. I just wanted you to have a little time of peace and quiet together. I thought—I hoped you might find things to say to each other. I also knew neither one of you would say a word to each other outside of polite niceties in any other environment."

Xanthe said incredulously, "You were matchmak-ing?"

"Maybe," said Niniane. She offered them a smile. "A little. Plus, I know you, Aubrey Riordan." She shook a finger at him. "If you had been home, you would have started back to work much too early, despite doctor's orders. So I made you stay here with lots of fresh air, good food and nothing more strenuous than a few games and some good books."

Aubrey scrubbed his face with both hands. After a moment he started to laugh. "Okay," he said. "Okay."

"Are you mad at me?" Niniane asked. "I can't tell."

"I don't know," he said. He dropped his hands and looked at Xanthe, who appeared to feel about as uncertain as he did. "I don't think so. Mostly I'm grateful. As long as you don't mind," he said to Xanthe.

She shook her head. "I'm grateful too."

"See, I told you it would all work out," Niniane said to Tiago.

"You are, as always, perfectly right," Tiago told her.

Tiago and Niniane stayed for a supper of grilled steaks, baked potatoes, salad greens and fresh pastries, and red wine. "You can come back home now, if you both want," Niniane said. She told Aubrey, "But if you do, you still can't go back to work for at least another sevenday."

He looked at Xanthe. "If I stay here, do I get to keep my nurse?"

Glee fizzed in Niniane's face. "Of course you do— that is, if she wants to stay too."

"Yes, Ma'am," said Xanthe, her lovely eyes smiling at Aubrey. "I would love to."

Niniane nodded. "Then that's settled."

Xanthe asked her, "How's Mouse, by the way?"

A shadow passed over Niniane's face and Aubrey frowned, bracing himself for bad news. "She's doing really well," Niniane said. "Her real name is Rachel. Her aunt and uncle have come to collect her, and they left for home yesterday."

"Why do you look sad?" he asked gently.

Niniane bit her lip as she stared at her plate. "I'm going to miss her."

Silence fell over the table. Children were, after all, rare enough gifts to the Elder Races. For Niniane and Tiago, the possibility of having children was nonexistent as long as she was Queen.

Aubrey set down his knife and fork as he looked around the table. Not so very long ago, he felt utterly bleak and betrayed, and so alone he would have welcomed death. Now sitting at the small table were the three people who meant the most to him. Blessings come in all ways, he thought, and they are always a surprise.

He raised his wine glass. "To new beginnings," he said as he looked at Xanthe. Her gaze lit until she looked luminous. "And to peace."

The others raised their glasses to clink with his.

Tiago said, "At least to peace for now."

Epilogue

The seven shrines of the gods were scattered all over Adriyel. Inanna's shrine lay four days' ride from the city.

Xanthe and Aubrey took the trip several moons later when the leaves started to turn in the autumn. Travel was pleasant in the cool, quiet days, and the nights had not yet grown unpleasantly cold.

They argued the whole way, even as they drew near to their destination.

"I wish you would listen to me when I say that I am content," Xanthe said.

"You may be content, but I am not," he said. "I do not see why you won't marry me."

"It's not fitting," she said stubbornly.

"Xanthe, you are the biggest snob I have ever met." His face was grim, and he looked quite forbidding. She found it almost unbearably sexy.

She glared at him. "Unfair! You know very well the more traditionally minded nobility would shun you if you married a commoner." She grimaced. "They are every bit as snobbish as I am, if not more."

"Fuck them," he snapped.

She clapped a hand over her mouth, not wanting to laugh. It was always so shocking whenever he cursed. He did it so seldom.

He was continuing. "Seriously. I don't care if it turns me into a pariah. If anybody is going to judge us on the merits of being married to each other, I don't want to socialize with them anyway."

"You have a point," she admitted with reluctance. She blew out a frustrated breath. "But I don't know how to be anything except a guard or an assassin."

He gave her a heated glance. "And now my lover."

She could hardly look at him and stay upright on her horse. He rode with immaculate, confident grace.

When they had returned to Adriyel, she had resumed her duties as one of Niniane's attendants and he as Chancellor, but they spent every night together at his house, and when she had her two days off, they went together to the cottage. Nights had become a golden time of enchantment and intimacy. Some days she could barely wait until the sun had set.

She whispered, "And that."

They rode in silence. Then he told her, "You would make a perfectly ferocious wife."

She widened her eyes. "I know! I would never be able to stop guarding you. I would be a social calamity."

"Did you ever stop to think," he said between his teeth, "that I might actually want and need a perfectly ferocious wife and social calamity. That is why I keep proposing to you."

She scrubbed at her forehead. "You're not going to give up, are you?"

"The only thing I am going to give up are my guards."

Incredulity sliced at her. She pulled her horse to a stop. "You can't."

"I absolutely can." He pulled his mount to a halt as well. His expression had turned hard and ruthless, and damn him, it made him even sexier than ever. "My guards don't do anything but follow me around and doze in the hallways when I work. At any rate, that attack on me was an aberration and it happened moons ago. Besides, I've got to find a way to blackmail you somehow."

"What are you talking about?" she shouted.

His eyebrows rose. In that moment he actually looked haughty. "If you won't marry me, I won't keep my guards. End of subject."

She exploded. "That's the stupidest thing I've ever heard!"

He nudged his horse forward, a smile playing around the corners of his lips. "It is so satisfying to dig underneath that calm façade of yours. I think it has become my second favorite pastime, my most favorite being when we make love, of course."

He kicked his horse into a canter, and she followed. "Get back here!"

"Darling, it is no use arguing about this any further," he called over his shoulder. "You know I will do exactly as I say, and Niniane will be so angry at you if I dismiss my guards."

"Aubrey!" Sending her own horse into a gallop, she caught up with him easily. "You leave Niniane out of this."

He looked entirely ruthless. "In fact as soon as we return, I plan on telling her how unhappy your refusal makes me. Her sympathies will not lie with you on this, Xanthe. Not when you are free to marry me if you would only choose to do so."

That struck her into silence, as he had known it would, for as long as Niniane remained the Dark Fae Queen, she and Tiago might be mated but they could never marry. Xanthe fumed and brooded as they rode into a small valley that was dotted with copses of trees crowned with the fiery colors of autumn.

They found the shrine at a crossroads. It was a simple affair, a grotto built of ancient stone beside a bubbling spring. They tethered their horses. Xanthe dug into one of her packs to retrieve the box of Tarot cards which she had wrapped in protective silk. Aubrey held his hand out to her, and she took it. They walked together to the shrine.

It was a peaceful place, silent except for the constant play of water falling over stone, deep with a sense of greening life despite winter's approach. Others had left offerings before them, a withered bouquet of flowers, fruit that had been nibbled at by wildlife and scattered on the ground, a tiny pair of knitted baby shoes. The sight of those caught at Xanthe, and she blinked back a sudden impulse to tears as she sent up a silent prayer for that unknown baby.

"I want to think that those shoes were left in gratitude for the birth of a new baby," she said in a husky voice. "And not because some child has passed."

Aubrey rubbed her back and said gently, "Then that is what we will believe."

As she glanced at him, he nodded an encouragement to her. She walked over and laid the box in the grotto. The mellow Power of the cards bathed her hands one last time as she let them go. *Thank you*, she said silently to the goddess. Like a chalice, her heart was filled to the brim. She had not known she could hold so much emotion.

In this quiet, eternal place, her arguments against marriage seemed superfluous, especially since she was arguing against her own wishes. She turned to Aubrey. "Yes, I'll marry you."

His face lit with triumph and joy. "I knew it," he said. He pulled her into his arms.

"Don't be insufferable about it," she told him, smiling. She laid her head on his shoulder.

He held her, his face buried in her hair. "You are the love of my life," he whispered. "That means I get to be as insufferable as I like."

"Oh, is that what it means?" She laughed and he chuckled too. She turned her face into his neck, her arms wrapped around his waist.

They stood together for a while as peace soaked into their bones. Then Aubrey kissed her temple. "Are you ready to start back?"

"Yes." She pulled away, glanced at the shrine—and froze as her world tilted.

The silk wrapped box had vanished.

She managed to whisper, "Aubrey."

"What?" He followed the direction of her gaze and stood very still, his expression sharp with wonder. "I'll be damned. It was hers."

"I thought—I mean, I guess I didn't really think it was true. Like you said, the chances of it were outrageously rare." She felt like she was babbling but she couldn't seem to stop. "What do you suppose will happen to it now?"

"She'll cast it into the world someplace else," Aubrey said. "Who knows when, or where?"

Xanthe smiled. "How lovely."

About the Author

Thea Harrison resides in Colorado. She wrote her first book, a romance, when she was nineteen and had sixteen romances published under the name Amanda Carpenter.

She took a break from writing to collect a couple of graduate degrees and a grown child. Her graduate degrees are in Philanthropic Studies and Library Information Science, but her first love has always been writing fiction. She's back with her paranormal Elder Races series. You can check out her website at: www.theaharrison.com, and also follow her on Twitter http://twitter.com/TheaHarrison and on Facebook at www.facebook.com/TheaHarrison. You can sign up for Thea's newsletter at http://theaharrison.com/contact-requests/.

Look for these titles from Thea Harrison

THE ELDER RACES SERIES
Published by Berkley

Dragon Bound

Half-human and half-wyr, Pia Giovanni spent her life keeping a low profile among the wyrkind and avoiding the continuing conflict between them and their Dark Fae enemies. But after being blackmailed into stealing a coin from the hoard of a dragon, Pia finds herself targeted by one of the most powerful–and passionate—of the Elder Races.

As the most feared and respected of the wyrkind, Dragos Cuelebre cannot believe someone had the audacity to steal from him, much less succeed. And when he catches the thief, Dragos spares her life, claiming her as his own to further explore the desire they've ignited in one another.

Storm's Heart
Serpent's Kiss
Oracle's Moon
Lord's Fall
Kinked

ELDER RACES NOVELLAS
Published by Samhain Publishing

True Colors
Natural Evil
Devil's Gate
Hunter's Season

AMANDA CARPENTER ROMANCES

Published by Samhain Publishing

A Deeper Dimension
The Wall
A Damaged Trust
The Great Escape
Flashback